Moonshadows

Praise for Melinda Hammond's *Moonshadows*

"...I didn't want to put the book down. Readers are sure to enjoy MOONSHADOWS."

~ *Marilyn Heyman, Romance Reviews today.*

"...This is an intriguing story, mixing the lives of two believable women. It makes for compelling reading and is beautifully told. The end is haunting and wholly satisfying. A book I thoroughly enjoyed!"

~ *Linda Sole, Red Roses for Authors*

Moonshadows

Melinda Hammond

A SAMHAIN PUBLISHING, LTD. publication.

Samhain Publishing, Ltd.
577 Mulberry Street, Suite 1520
Macon, GA 31201
www.samhainpublishing.com

Moonshadows
Copyright © 2009 by Melinda Hammond
Print ISBN: 978-1-60504-325-8
Digital ISBN: 1-60504-188-2

Editing by Deborah Nemeth
Cover by Angela Waters

First Samhain Publishing, Ltd. electronic publication: September 2008
First Samhain Publishing, Ltd. print publication: July 2009

Dedication

For TGH

Chapter One

Night. Black, and wet. She was standing before a pair of tall gates, the bars intertwined with gleaming rose briars, cunningly wrought from the same unyielding iron as the gates themselves. She tried to open them, but they wouldn't move, and she was overwhelmed with a fear and anxiety so great it paralysed her limbs and left her stomach churning as it roused her from her dreams. Then the moment was gone and she drifted away again, unable to decide whether she was trying to get out of the gates, or to get in.

The insistent bleeping of the alarm dragged Jez from her deep sleep. With one deft movement her fingers pressed the snooze button and she turned over. Another ten minutes, then she would get up. Her mind clung to the remnants of a pleasant dream: glittering lights, the buzz and chatter of a hundred voices...

London, 1746

The room was hot and crowded. Dozens of candles flickered from the chandeliers, their flames reflected in the highly polished lustres and shining on the brightly coloured silks and brocades of the assembly. Sarah fanned herself nervously. The new, stiffly padded gown with its wide hoops and low-cut

9

neckline felt heavy and uncomfortable. As she passed a mirror, she glanced at her reflection and a stranger stared back at her, the face a white-painted mask and her hair, usually a soft reddish-gold, curled and grey-pomaded specially for the occasion. Only her clear green eyes were unchanged. She clung even tighter to Thomas' arm.

"Heavens, my dear. Have a care, you are crushing my new figured velvet." He smiled down at her. "There is no need to be nervous, Sarah. You are not the first young woman to be presented to His Majesty, although I don't doubt you are one of the most handsome."

She forced a smile to her own lips, grateful for her husband's clumsy attempt at a compliment. Dear Thomas. He himself had only been to Court once before, yet he was anxious to put her at her ease.

"Come." He led her forward. "It is time to make your curtsey to your King."

Her knees were shaking so much that she thought she might fall, but somehow she managed to walk in line into the chamber and to make her low curtsey with tolerable composure. It was over in seconds and the procession carried them out through the double doors into the grand salon.

"There my dear, that was not so bad!" remarked Thomas. "Why, madam, you are still trembling. Now, you must wait there, and I will bring you a glass of negus. That will make you feel more the thing, eh, my love?"

"Oh no, no, pray don't leave me," she whispered.

"Now, now, my dear, do not be a silly puss." Patting her hand, he walked off in search of refreshment.

Sarah watched him go, her fingers clenched nervously on the sticks of her fan. Thomas disappeared into the crowd and

Sarah looked anxiously around her at the noisy, jostling crowds. She felt very alone and out of place. Some of the gentlemen glanced towards her, their faces expressing only haughty indifference, and one heavily bejeweled lady subjected her to a long, disapproving stare. Disconcerted, Sarah stepped back a pace, only to feel her heel come down upon a foot.

"Oh—I am so sorry." She swept round and her heavy skirts threatened to throw her off balance but the gentleman behind her put out a steadying hand.

"There is no harm done. Pray, madam, do not distress yourself. Come, I think you should sit down."

"Oh thank you. I do beg your pardon, sir, so stupid of me. It is all so new, you see, and there are so many people—"

He sat down beside her and, taking the fan from her agitated fingers, flicked it open and began to fan her gently. She stole a glance up at him. A handsome face, she thought, with a firm jaw and finely cut features, but under the fashionable white maquillage he looked faintly bored. At that moment his dark eyes met her anxious look and he smiled, softening the rather harsh lines of his countenance. Sarah found herself smiling back, relieved to find a friendly face in a room full of haughty strangers.

"It is your first time at Court, madam?"

"Yes. I was so nervous, I thought I might faint," she confided. "My husband brought me to Town that I might be presented, but you see I have never quit Burford before—we live so quietly at home that I had no idea everything would be so, so magnificent!"

"It occurs to me you do not mean that as a compliment."

"Oh, I meant no disrespect, but when one has been used to family parties and the occasional assembly, to be suddenly thrust into society is quite—quite *daunting*, especially amongst

11

so many strangers."

"But they will not be strangers for long, madam. Soon you will come to recognise them and then they will not frighten you."

"Is that truly so, sir? Do you know everyone here?"

"In the main, yes."

She leaned towards him, her shyness forgotten. "Then pray tell me, sir, do you know the lady over there? The dark-eyed lady with the brown hair. How strange she looks, yet everyone seems to be paying court to her. Is she a relative of the king?"

"No, madam, that is the Walmoden. I perceive from your blank look that you have no idea of what I am saying to you." He looked amused. "What an innocent you are! It is the Countess Walmoden, the King's mistress."

Her eyes widened. She stared again at the plump little woman in the heavily laced mantua.

"He has others, of course, but she is his chief preoccupation."

"Well, that merely confirms—no, I must not comment." She closed her lips.

"I wish you would."

"Forgive me, sir. This is your society and I know very little of it. It does not behove me to be disparaging, but—I *cannot* approve."

"Alas, madam, it is the way of the world."

"Then I think I should prefer to be at home and to keep the society of my close friends and neighbours." She smiled ruefully. "I have no doubt you find my country notions quite nonsensical, for I can see that you are quite at home here amongst these crowds."

"Yet I too prefer small parties."

"Just so. But I would not for the world have Thomas think that I am not entertained. He has only recently become a baronet, you see. Quite unexpected, for no-one could know that his brother Edmund would break his neck on the hunting field. And Thomas says it is our duty now to spend a season in Town, to acquire a little polish, but it seems such an expense to me, when there is so much at home that needs attention. Why, the cost of this gown alone would have paid for a new roof on the stables. Oh dear!" She clapped her hands to her mouth, trying to stifle the laugh that was bubbling up inside her. "I should not be talking so to you, sir, for you are a complete stranger to me. Forgive me."

"No, no, I am honoured that you should confide in me."

"Well that is just the thing, you see. I do not know why it should be, but I do feel that I can talk to you, as if I had known you forever. But that is no reason why my tongue should run on like a fiddlestick, until you are quite *sick* with boredom."

"Oh I assure you, madam, I am not at all bored. I find you quite charming."

"Do you? How kind of you to say so. I do not chatter on like this at home, you see, but then, when one is amongst friends, everything is so much more comfortable, do you not agree?"

"I've no idea. You see, I have no friends."

"But you said you knew most of those here."

"Ah, but that does not mean they are my *friends*. Acquaintances merely, and the rest—lovers, and enemies."

Sarah stared at the gentleman, wondering if he was joking her, but before she could think of a reply Sir Thomas came up to them.

"Your wine, my dear. My apologies for leaving you so long." He glared at her companion, who had risen to his feet, smiling faintly as he handed the fan back to Sarah. As he bowed she

13

noticed in his closeness the faint, pleasant scent of sandalwood.

"I am now *de trop* here. Your servant, madam, sir." He sauntered away, leaving Sir Thomas seething with indignation.

"Of all the coxcombs, playing off his airs upon you—was he offensive, my dear? I've a mind to call him out."

"No, no, not at all. His only offence was that we are not introduced, so I have no idea who he is—a friend of yours, perhaps, sir?"

"Friend? Good God no!"

"No of course," she murmured, her eyes twinkling as she remembered the stranger's words. "An acquaintance, perhaps?"

"I don't consider him even that, and when I saw the fellow talking to you I hurried back as quick as ever I could, I can tell you. You must stay away from him, Sarah. Dashed dangerous fellow."

"Oh? He did not tell me his name...?"

"The Earl of Cordeaux. Fabulously wealthy, of course, and thinks he can ride roughshod over everyone. You probably found him a little too forward."

"No, not at all, I found him very—polite." She was going to say charming, but some instinct warned her to play down the gentleman's attentions. She glanced across the room to where the earl was standing with his back to her. Tall, elegant and with a hint of insouciance about him—so different from her own stolid husband.

She slept late the next morning and was roused by the maid throwing open the shutters of her bedroom. She sat up in bed and, as Hannah put down the tray with her cup of hot chocolate, she gasped.

There beside her cup was a small nosegay of spring flowers

and a card inscribed with the name of Cordeaux...

§

"Jez—wake up, sleepy head. Come on, you're working today."

She groaned and opened her eyes to find Harry sitting on the edge of the bed.

"Never mind, at least it's Friday—the end of your first week as a working woman. Brought you a coffee." He bent to kiss her, one hand caressing her breast. "Mm, you smell nice—flowery—a new perfume?" She arched towards him for a moment, then turned away from his roving fingers and struggled to sit up.

"Don't be silly—I haven't put any perfume on yet. And if I have to get to work, then there's no time for *that*!" She sipped at the coffee. "Lord, I feel odd—you know, when you've been dreaming and wake up and can't remember what it was...you want to go back to sleep to finish it off."

"No, I don't think I've ever felt that."

She threw him a scornful glance. "Then you have no soul." She drained her mug and jumped out of bed. "Bags I have the shower first!"

When she emerged from the shower he handed her the refilled mug.

"So tell me again how long you will be working at CME?"

"Oh Harry, don't you ever listen? It's a six-month secondment to the company, three days a week. The brief is to study their business practices and make judgements and recommendations—I'll still have to go to the university every week and my report will be assessed as part of my MSc. I was so lucky to get in at CME, it's the cream of the placements—

they rarely take anyone."

"And you're getting paid?"

"No—well, there's a nominal wage."

Harry grunted. "Slave labour. Of course they were willing to take you on."

She put her arms around him. "Don't worry, Harry. When I've finished I'll be able to get a real job, and hopefully one that pays well. Then I can start to put more into the household kitty. 'Til then we'll just have to keep a tight rein on the spending."

"So what's new?" He kissed her nose. "Don't worry, love. I know you're doing your best—and you *are* providing the cottage—or at least your mother is. Now, out of the way so I can shower."

Dear Harry, he was so supportive. "You've got a good brain," he kept telling her. "You have to use it."

Well, they'd survived this long. Only another nine months and she'd be free to make some real money, instead of working two evenings a week as a waitress to supplement her income. She glanced at the clock—Christ, she was daydreaming again. She dragged her most businesslike suit out of the wardrobe— short skirt and jacket in sage green, which reflected the colour of her eyes.

"How long does it take you to get there?" Harry asked as he came into the bedroom.

"It's the other side of Filchester...half-hour, twenty minutes if the traffic's light."

He whistled as he watched her struggle into a pair of tights.

"Damn. Now I've put my finger through them!" She inspected the damage, then continued to pull them on. "It's only at the top, so no-one will see it, and besides, I can't find another pair." She zipped up the skirt, scraped back her unruly red hair into a knot and put on a pair of black-rimmed glasses.

"No contact lenses today?"

"I thought the glasses would look better—more professional."

Harry grinned as he looked her up and down. "I think you look sexy—like a schoolmistress."

"That's not the idea."

"I know, but I like it."

"I want to look the part today—I've got to talk to Lavinia Woods, the Marketing Manager. She seems to think that this placement is for an office junior. My access to information is limited to the really basic level and the most difficult task I've done so far is keying in customers' details into a database."

"I know, you told me all this last night." He put his arms around her. "Go sock it to 'em, kid."

Jez drove to the CME building in determined mood. She would speak to Lavinia. After all, she was a twenty-four year-old graduate working for her degree, not a sixteen-year-old school-leaver. The car park was unusually full, but she managed to find a space then walked into the building with her head high. As soon as the morning briefing was over, she approached the manager's desk.

"Lavinia? I think there's something we need to discuss."

"Oh, Jez—thank heaven! I've the most horrendous problem—I've a meeting with the board this morning and I've left *all* the copies of my report at home except this one. Could you be *a real star* and copy it for me? I only need ten copies, but I haven't quite finished the budget breakdown for this half-year, and if I break off now...well, you know what I mean. Sorry to drop this on you, Jessica, but I would be *so* grateful."

17

The saccharine smile could not have been sweeter. Jez knew that she should refuse, but if Lavinia *was* about to go into an important meeting, she certainly would not be able to apply her mind to anyone else's problems. With a tight little smile, Jez took the sheaf of papers and went to the document room. This was little more than an alcove off the main office containing various printers and copiers. Lavinia's assistant, Melanie, had shown her how to use the copier on the first day.

"It couldn't be simpler," she had said. "Just put in your original and follow the instructions on the screen. Tell the machine what you want it to do. Easy."

Such statements made Jez wary but it had looked pretty simple when Melanie demonstrated. Jez put the originals into the tray and keyed in ten copies. She pressed the start button and immediately the copier burst into life, swallowing the originals and churning out printed copies at top speed.

Unfortunately, the print was so tiny it was almost illegible.

"Oh shit!" Jez sprang towards the machine. As she did so her hand dislodged the output tray, which crashed to the floor, followed by the copies that were now spewing out of the copier. "Shit, shit shit!" she muttered, desperately pushing at the buttons. It made no difference; the copies still kept coming. "You stupid machine, stop."

"Here, let me." A hand moved past her and pressed a small red button. The copier stopped.

Jez stared at the console where the hand still rested, a heavy gold signet ring adorning one of the long, tapering fingers.

"Phew! Thank you, it—it sort of, ran away with me..." Jez turned and found herself staring at a wall of dark blue. As her brain adjusted to the view she realised she was looking at the breast pocket of a suit. A man's suit. Her eyes travelled upwards past the immaculate pale blue shirt and dark silk tie to the face, where she found herself gazing into a pair of deep blue eyes.

They gleamed with amusement—not laughing at her but smiling, inviting her to share the joke. The owner of the blue eyes was standing so close that Jez could feel the charm radiating from him and she was aware of a faint tang of spicy aftershave in the air. In a split second she had registered the whole person: tall enough to be striking, raven-black hair and with the sort of tan gained on the ski slopes rather than the beach. He had the lean, clean-cut features she had always thought attractive, with just enough ruggedness to prevent them being too perfect. He also looked vaguely familiar, although she could not place him.

He smiled. "Life runs away with all of us at some time."

Jez found her toes curling at the deep, mellow voice. She realised she was smiling back at him in a most idiotic way and she frantically cudgelled her brains for something to say. She swallowed hard and nervously adjusted her glasses.

"I—I need ten copies of this report..."

He scooped up a pile of copies the machine had already thrown out. "Looks like someone left the machine set to reduce the copy. We'll cancel that and set it to collate and staple for you as well."

As he fixed the output tray back into place, Jez collected up the rest of the ruined sheets, wondering how many trees she had just wasted. While he was busy with the controls, she took another look at her rescuer. Early thirties, she guessed, expensively dressed—probably a director, here for the board meeting. That could be useful...

She found herself once more under the scrutiny of those blue eyes.

"I've not seen you before. You must be new."

Jez decided this chance was too good to miss. She switched on a brilliant smile and held out her hand, adopting what she hoped was a friendly but businesslike tone.

"Jez Skelton. I'm studying for my degree at the university— Master of Sciences specialising in business and marketing techniques. I'm here for a few months to study the company, but Lavinia seems to think I should start right at the bottom."

"Giving you the menial tasks, is she? Vinnie's very good at that."

"I suppose it is useful to know how to frank the mail and use the copier, but on my current performance I'm not going to get far in six months."

He laughed, and Jez felt as if a sackful of butterflies had been released in her stomach.

"So what should you be doing here?"

"I'm just completing the last module of the course, market analysis and strategy for winning business. I was lucky to get this placement. All the students were after it—after all, Cordeaux Manufacturing Enterprises was started from scratch five years ago and now turnover is around twenty million, so it must be doing *something* right."

"You've done your homework."

"No point in going into business if you don't."

"True. Your copies are done. Here, take them. And don't worry, you'll soon get the hang of it. See you later."

Jez watched him stroll away. *Oh I hope so.*

Chapter Two

Jez sat at her desk, staring at the monitor. Lavinia had taken her report and rushed off to her meeting, too busy to do more than ask her to continue adding more names to the mailing list database. She wondered if the man she had met in the document room would put in a good word for her. He had probably forgotten all about her now, and she would just have to tackle Lavinia herself when she got back.

Jez had just made herself a coffee when the Marketing Manager returned to her office, followed by the man himself. As they passed the desk, Lavinia stopped.

"And this is Jessica Skelton, the student I mentioned. Jessica, this is Piers Cordeaux."

Jez almost dropped her coffee. How could she have been so dumb? She had been chatting up the owner of the company and not even known it.

He gave no indication that they had met before, but she knew he had not missed her startled reaction and for a few seconds he held her glance, a wicked gleam in his own. "Hi, Jessica." He paused. "What do your friends call you?"

"Jez..."

"Ah, Jez. Yes. Vinnie tells me you're with us for a few months. You're in luck, you know. We are just beginning a big push to launch our new security software package. So far all we have is the product and the name, Sentinel, so you'll be able to sit in with Vinnie on tomorrow's briefing meeting with our advertising agents. Isn't that right, Vinnie?"

"Of course, Piers..."

"And perhaps we can arrange a trip to Cordeaux House for you—that's our London office—it'll give you a better idea of how this section fits into our overall organisation."

"Thank you. I should like that, very much."

"Well!" When Piers had walked away, Lavinia Woods tapped her pen on the desk in a thoughtful tattoo. "He's in a good mood, today. He's normally out of here as soon as the meeting's over. Of course, I've been telling the board for ages that we need to encourage fresh ideas within the company."

Melanie, the office assistant, was more forthcoming. Word soon spread around the office that the Great Man had spoken to Jessica. She was not surprised to find her female companions were all drooling over Piers Cordeaux.

"But he's just gorgeous," explained Melanie, hitching up her skirt and perching on the corner of Jessica's desk. "All the girls have the hots for him and it's not just good looks. He is *always* nice to everyone."

"I suppose that's easy when everyone does what you want all the time."

Melanie gave a huge sigh. "You just wait 'til he gives you that come-to-bed look—unfortunately it never goes any further. I think he's got some rule about not mixing business with pleasure. And then again, why should he bother with us when he can have any girl he wants? You only have to look in the papers to see the sort of girls he takes out—tall leggy blondes, actresses and models—we don't have a chance."

Jez didn't like to admit that she could not remember seeing a picture of Piers with any girl. But then, the photos she had seen of him were in the *FT* or the *Economist,* indistinct group shots of suited businessmen, which would explain why she had not recognised him.

Melanie was still talking. "And he wears that lovely woody after-shave. Lavinia knows what it is, Safari or something. And it's not expensive, at least not when you think that he can afford to buy whatever he wants. But then, Piers is like that, he doesn't flash his money around, showing off his Our Man suits and things—"

"Don't you mean Armani?" Jez smiled.

"Yeah, something like that. No designer labels or huge gold bracelets that say 'look at me, I'm rich.' Not showy, you know what I mean?"

"I do." Jez hesitated, then gave in to base curiosity. "But if he's so attractive, and he's not gay, why isn't he married?"

"He was once." Melanie leafed through the pile of papers in her hand. "Divorced now. No kids." She sighed. "He built CME from nothing, owns a string of hotels, several other companies, charters yachts for cruises in the Med—all that living and only thirty-five." She cast an anxious look at Jessica. "That's not too old for me, is it?"

Jez laughed. "Far too old. Just think, when you're forty he'll be nearly sixty."

Melanie's wistful look changed into a grin. "Yeah, you're right. And he's not the sort you could take clubbin' with your mates, is he?"

The next day was wet, but even the continuous rain could not dampen Jessica's enthusiasm. At last she was going to see the real work of the marketing department. By lunchtime her head was buzzing with slogans and possible advertising campaigns. The girl from the agency had been very friendly and had even suggested that she put forward a few points for discussion.

Jez was so engrossed in writing up her notes that she did not notice everyone else had left, so it was nearly six o'clock when she walked across the car park to her aged car. She wanted to fly home to tell Harry about her day. Reality kicked in with a jolt when the car failed to start. She turned the key again but nothing happened. For a few dazed moments, she stared out through the windscreen. It was raining heavily now, and there were only a few cars left in the car park, none of them belonging to anyone she knew. She looked at her watch. Harry would be travelling home—no point in trying to contact him for an hour at least.

With a sigh she pulled her case off the back seat and stepped out into the rain. It was not cold, but her light cotton suit offered little protection from the rain, and it was soon seeping through to her shoulders. Keeping her head down, she set off at a brisk pace towards the bus stop.

"Can I give you a lift anywhere?"

She jumped as the black Porsche slid up beside her.

Piers Cordeaux reached across and opened the door. "Get in. I'm sure the leather will take a little damp."

She hesitated, then lowered herself into the seat, wincing a little as her wet suit pressed against her. As she closed the door she became aware of the sensuous smell of the leather upholstery.

"Thanks. My car died on me." She pushed the wet tendrils of hair from her face. "I'll come back later with a friendly mechanic."

"You look different today. I know—no glasses."

She grinned. "Contact lenses. I'm a slave to vanity."

"You shouldn't worry about it—the glasses looked good. Where am I taking you?"

Jez swallowed hard, and not knowing how to respond to the compliment, she ignored it. "I want to go to Luxbury, but you could drop me at the central bus station—"

"Wouldn't dream of it. I'll head that way and you can direct me."

"But aren't you going back to London? That's the other direction."

"No problem. It won't take long."

"Then thank you." She glanced at him. "My homework wasn't as thorough as it should have been. I didn't know who you were when I bent your ear yesterday."

"No." He grinned. "I guessed as much from your expression when Vinnie introduced me. How's it been today?"

"Fantastic. I joined the brainstorming session this morning, and they are even letting me put in a few of my ideas—that is— you didn't tell them to do that, did you?"

"No. Scout's honour. If they are considering your ideas, it's because you made an impression on them, too."

She was too busy with her own thoughts to realise the significance of the last little word.

"Oh, wow. I don't suppose they'll use them, but it's nice to know they're taking me seriously." She glanced around her. "This is beautiful. Company car?"

"One of them. Actually it was chosen by the sales director. Ex-sales director."

"Oh? He's no longer with you?"

"She. No, she had to go. That's why I've become more involved in the business again, until I can find a replacement. And the replacement gets the car."

25

Jez wondered about the unfortunate sales director. Curiosity overcame her. "Did you get rid of her? Why, what did she do?"

"More a case of what she didn't do. She wasn't up to the job. And she talked out of turn."

"Did she kiss and tell?" Jez regretted the words as soon as they were uttered, and his impatient look told her she'd made a mistake.

His reply was short. "There was no kissing, and nothing to tell. We didn't agree on policy."

She coloured, wishing to be anywhere but in the confined space of the car. But when Piers Cordeaux spoke again there was nothing but polite curiosity in his tone.

"How long have you lived in Luxbury?"

"About ten years. My mother moved into Lilac Cottage after Father died. I chose to go to the university here, so when Mother remarried and moved to Spain, she let me stay on at the cottage."

"That was fortunate. What was your degree course?"

"Philosophy."

"Hell! What did that teach you?"

She laughed. "To argue."

He grinned, but did not speak, concentrating instead on negotiating a busy roundabout.

"I suppose, if you're local, you'll know Kitty's restaurant. I'm told it's very good."

"Yes, I believe it is, though I've never been there."

"Maybe you'd like to eat there with me tonight."

Jez froze. She was surprised by the invitation but even more so as she realised that she was momentarily tempted. "I'm sorry. It's not possible. I'm in a relationship, you see."

"Of course. I should have guessed." He did not sound disappointed, which Jez found mildly irritating. "Tell me about your partner—another student?"

"Harry? No. He's an engineer, only on the first rung of the ladder, of course, but he's very ambitious, and loving every minute of it," she added proudly, then blushed. Piers Cordeaux could not possibly wish to know about Harry.

"No plans to settle down then."

"Not until I've established my own career."

"Very wise. This is Luxbury High Street, I think—where now?"

"That row of cottages on the left—Lilac Cottage is the one on the end. Seems a pretty odd name now, but I suppose once it looked out onto the village green."

He drew up smoothly and she thanked him again for the lift.

"No problem. I hope you enjoy your work with CME, Jez. 'Bye."

As he pulled away a group of young boys in the bus shelter opposite stared at the car then cast curious glances towards her. It was still raining, and she felt slightly cold after the warmth of the Porsche, but it did not bother her. She felt good—well, it wasn't every day that a multi-millionaire asked her out to dinner.

When Harry got home, she told him about her car. He predicted a flat battery and drove her back to collect it.

"There, told you," he said, removing the jump leads once the Vauxhall's engine was running. "You probably left your lights on this morning. God-awful day, though. How did you get home?"

"Oh—one of the guys from the office gave me a lift."

She quashed her conscience. No point in going into detail, she told herself. No reason to complicate matters.

However, she could not resist mentioning the incident to Kate when they met for lunch the following week. Jez had always thought of Kate as her best friend. They had known each other since school and, although Kate was a couple of years older than Jez, they had kept in touch over the years. Kate was a solicitor in Filchester, where she was working hard to make a name for herself. She told Jez she would treat her to lunch to celebrate being made a junior partner in the firm of Milton, Chilton and Didcot. "How about you, Jez, what's new with you?"

Jez considered and decided that Piers' invitation was the most interesting thing that had happened to her for some time. When Kate heard about it she turned her huge baby-blue eyes on her friend.

"You turned him down? What's wrong with him?"

"Nothing, if you like them tall, dark, rich and good-looking." It was as much as Jez could do to stifle a sigh. "But I'm with Harry now."

"Yes, but there's no harm in trying out a new model occasionally."

"You make it sound like choosing a new car." Jez laughed, but Kate spread her hands and shrugged.

"And why not? Get what you can out of life, that's my motto."

Kate always had a different man in tow, which did not surprise Jez. Kate had a model's figure, perfect features and long honey-blond hair that fell over her shoulders like a silk curtain. When Kate had walked into the little restaurant, the men's heads had turned to look at her. There were always plenty of men waiting to take her out, but no one special. Kate always said she'd know when she met Mr. Right—there would be bells, bright lights and fireworks.

"I'm happy with Harry."

Kate rolled her eyes and helped herself to the salad. "My God! You sound like you're resigning yourself to the consolation prize."

"Don't be stupid."

"You think you and Harry are going to be together for life?"

"Yes."

"So where's the fireworks? I know it's corny but does the earth move for you?"

Jez picked at her lasagne. "Sort of..."

Kate put down her fork and stared at her friend. "There's no *sort of* about it. When someone presses the right buttons for you, you'll know it."

Jez laughed. "That doesn't sound very romantic. Besides, there's more to a relationship than sex, Kate. Harry and I have a lot in common."

Kate looked sceptical, so to prevent an argument Jez quickly changed the subject, but the conversation stuck in her mind, unsettling her. Perhaps she and Harry had got into a rut recently. But they were happy together and you couldn't expect the same excitement as at the very beginning of a relationship. After all, they had been together for eighteen months...

Chapter Three

Jez heard nothing from Piers Cordeaux during the next two weeks but he remained in her thoughts, and when Lavinia said she could come to the forthcoming software exhibition in Birmingham she wondered if he had suggested it. Yet how could she pass up such an opportunity?

"So you're leaving me for a week." Harry nuzzled her neck as they lay in bed together that night.

"No, it's only three days."

"Staying in a hotel—it'll be like a holiday."

She giggled. "I know, I can hardly wait."

"And what am I going to do without you?" he murmured, nibbling her ear.

She turned towards him and pressed her body against his.

"I'll have to give you something to think about while I'm gone."

Jez travelled to the National Exhibition Centre in Birmingham with Lavinia and Dave Kent, the sales manager. They were meeting the sales team on the stand at four o'clock for a pre-show briefing. She was quite bewildered by the acres of car parking space and enormous exhibition halls, and when they eventually reached their stand her feet were aching—she made a mental note to wear something comfortable the following day.

In the large, echoing exhibition hall contractors were putting the finishing touches to the stand, a dazzling construction of chrome and royal blue, erecting the huge signs and spotlights that would bring a touch of showbiz glamour. Dave introduced her to the team before running through the product and sales pitch. He had to raise his voice against the noise of the workmen on the other stands, and the background pop music that was playing constantly.

When the discussions grew technical she found her attention wandering and was pleased when Piers Cordeaux arrived, looking cool and relaxed in a soft blue shirt and superbly cut jeans. She admired the way he talked to the team, encouraging them, addressing a positive comment to each one of them, making them feel that they mattered. She had to admit he knew how to handle people.

By five o'clock everything was ready. Jez had sorted and stored the sales literature and checked the hospitality area while Lavinia tried out the demonstration software. Even Jez was aware of her colleagues' buzz of excitement; they were all keen to be there for the start of the exhibition.

"Well, that's all, folks." Dave rubbed his hands together. "Let's get back to the Oaks and you can all go over your notes before dinner."

"Make sure you are all here, nine-thirty sharp and raring to go," added Piers.

"Just a moment." Lavinia was sorting through her papers. "I don't seem to have a booking here for you, Jessica. I'd better check with Drina."

Jez looked at Dave. "Who's Drina?"

"Piers' PA. She runs the London office and organises all

this."

Lavinia stood with the telephone to her ear, frowning. "I know it was short notice, but—okay, okay, I'll tell her. 'Bye." She switched off the phone. "She couldn't get another room at the Oaks, you know what it's like when there are so many exhibitions on here. She finally found you a room at the Manor."

Dave whistled. "Nothing but the best, eh Jez? Lucky girl."

Piers stepped forward. "That's where I'm staying. You'd better come back with me."

Jez was immediately suspicious. She followed Piers to the Porsche, retrieving her case from Lavinia's Mondeo on the way. He opened the boot of the car and slid his briefcase into the small gap beside his own luggage.

"Will I have to keep my case on my knees?" she asked, her eyes twinkling mischievously.

"No. There's room in the front." He opened the bonnet and she stared at the carpeted space.

"Where's the engine?"

It was his turn to smile. "The Boxter's a mid-engined model. It's there, behind the seats."

"But how do you get to it?"

"You don't. There are two plastic caps for the water and the oil in the boot. Anything else, you call the dealer."

"How fantastic—I want one."

He laughed at that. "Come on, let's get to the hotel."

As the others drove away, Jez wanted to ask Piers if he had planned this, but could not bring herself to do so. Instead she kept a reserved silence as they drove through the lanes to the hotel. Stealing a glance at his profile, she thought he looked anything but happy with the arrangement.

"I hope this isn't spoiling your plans."

"No, but you may have to eat alone tonight. I've a previous engagement with the head of Blue Chip Computers. Sorry."

He didn't sound it. She shrugged. "That's fine. I'll manage."

It was growing dark when they left the motorway. Piers threaded the Porsche through the busy streets, turning off into a narrow tree-lined lane that twisted through the darkness.

"Ah. Here we are."

Piers pulled onto a gravel drive that led through the gateway to the hotel. After the modern lines of the Exhibition Centre and the busy motorway traffic, Jez was unprepared for the hotel. The house was directly before them, floodlit through the trees. She gasped and blinked. Could she really be staying here?

The Old Manor was a beautiful country house with deep gables and mullioned windows flanking the central porch. Situated on a slight rise, the house towered above them as they approached the entrance, the golden stonework gleaming against the black backdrop of the night sky.

"It's beautiful," she breathed. "Elizabethan?"

"Yes. At least, externally. Most of the interior dates from the eighteenth century, but thankfully it also has some very modern features."

"Like the helipad over there." Jez grinned. "We could have avoided the traffic by flying in."

"Mm, I've done that in the past but I prefer to drive."

Jez squirmed inwardly. *Oh my God.* Was he really that rich?

§

In the ballroom, Lady Marcham watched the entrance of a young couple, a faint smile curling her painted lips. Cousin Thomas' ruddy cheek and brown frock coat might shout of the country, but little Sarah's sack-backed gown of canary yellow silk with its blond lace trimming and embroidered petticoat could not be faulted. She heard a noise behind her and turned to see a lady in a lime green robe come in from the terrace. The lady paused by the window, fanning herself rapidly before hurrying away into the crowd. A moment later another figure strolled in—a gentleman in a powder blue frock coat generously laced with gold. He hesitated on the threshold, shaking out the snow-white ruffles at his wrist while he surveyed the assembly.

Lady Marcham shut her fan and used it to beckon the gentleman towards her. "Richard, my dear—the very person I need."

"Always happy to be of service, madam."

"Nonsense, sir—you know you never put yourself out for anyone," she retorted. Her eyes narrowed as she spotted a small black crescent at one corner of his mouth. "And you have taken to wearing a patch. Another affectation, Richard?"

"But of course. It is all the rage, my dear. I call this one the, ah, *Dangereuse*."

"Very apt—for you. But I digress. I want to introduce you to a young cousin of mine. Fresh from the country and knows not a soul. You will dance with her, Richard."

"Oh dear, must I? Country maids are not at all in my line, you know."

"I am well aware of that, which is the reason I may safely present her to you. She's well enough, but not at all in your line, thank Heaven!" She intercepted his glance towards the lady in lime green and tapped his arm sharply with her fan. "If you are going to cuckold Spenningham, sir, pray do not do so in my house."

"Too late, I fear." His dark eyes mocked her. "Jealous, madam?"

"Not a bit. Our brief liaison was delightful, Richard dear, but I am well aware of your need for constant variety. Come, I will introduce you to my little cousin."

"But what if she falls in love with me?" he said as they made their way across the room.

"She won't. Sarah is a clergyman's daughter with very strict ideas of morality."

"And why should you trouble yourself over a little country cousin, my lady?"

"Because she is a sweet little thing and I want her to enjoy her visit to London. God knows when she will get another. Thomas will incarcerate her in the country, where she will be expected to run his house and bear more children." She broke off as they approached Sarah, who was sitting alone in a little alcove, watching the dancing and tapping one dainty foot to the music.

"Sarah, my love, has Thomas deserted you already?"

The young lady rose, smiling. "He is in the card room, cousin, but I assure you I do not mind at all."

"But it will not do. You must dance, and I have here the perfect partner. Lady Methven, will you allow me to present the Earl of Cordeaux."

Sarah curtseyed and held out her hand. "I know—that is, we have not been introduced, but we have *spoken*," she said with a sunny smile. "You may not remember me sir, for I was painted up like a doll on that occasion, and my curls were powdered."

The earl raised her fingers to his lips, his eyes taking in the abundant flame-coloured hair curling about her head. "I remember perfectly, madam, and may I say I very much prefer your natural colouring. Now that the formalities have been observed, will you do me the honour of dancing with me?"

"Of course, my lord. I should be delighted to dance—only, you will forgive me if I am a little nervous..."

Smiling, Lady Marcham watched them walk away. Having done her duty by her little cousin, she was now free to enjoy herself.

"You dance well, sir."

The earl's lips twitched. His partners usually waited for *him* to pay the compliments.

"Thank you. How do you like London?"

"Very much, but I do miss the children."

"That is not very fashionable."

She laughed. "But I am not fashionable. I had much rather be at home with my little ones. You see, Jenny is only three, and little Thomas is but two years old, and I miss them so."

"Why did you not bring them with you?"

"Oh I so wanted to, my lord, but Sir Thomas says London is such a sinful, unhealthy place and that they are much better with their nurse in the country. And I confess that now I have been about Town a little, I think he is quite correct. That is, they would be in danger from infection—I do not *think* there is any danger of such little ones being corrupted, do you?"

The movement of the dance separated them before he could reply.

"Do you think us so immoral then, here in Town?" he said as they came back together.

"My lord?"

"You said London was a sinful, unhealthy place."

"Oh dear, I have offended you. I mean—that is—I know nothing of you personally, sir, but—but I understand that the metropolis is a very wicked place."

"Perhaps my Lady Marcham ought to have warned you, madam, that I am one of her more—ah—*wicked* guests."

She stared at him, her embarrassment apparently forgotten. "No, are you? What have you done? No, no I am sorry. I should not have asked that." She blushed rosily, then, stealing a glance at her companion, she gave a sigh of relief. "You are teasing me. Thank goodness—I feared my unruly tongue had offended you." She regarded him thoughtfully and when he smiled, her own eyes twinkled with mischief and a dimple peeped at the corner of her mouth. "Pray do not answer if you do not wish to, my lord, but people *have* told me you are dangerous. Have you—have you fought a duel?"

"Dozens of 'em!"

"And"—her tone was hushed—"and have you ever…killed your opponent?"

"Yes, upon several occasions. Does that shock you? You asked me the question."

"I know. It was very wrong of me, only—no-one else would tell me the truth. It is all hints and whispers—how I detest such roundaboutation."

"So too do I, madam." He watched her thoughtful countenance. "Have they also hinted that I am notorious for seducing other men's wives? There, madam, you stare at me. Are you a little frightened of me now?"

To his surprise she laughed merrily. "No, why should I be? *I* am in no danger from you."

"You think not?"

"I know it," she replied firmly. "*Your* taste, my lord, is not hinted at, but loudly proclaimed. You like only the most beautiful women. For example, the lady in the lime green robe who is watching us so intently."

The earl threw back his head and laughed, startling the other dancers, who looked around to see who had dared to disturb their elegant murmurings.

"Lady Methven, you are a gem, a treasure!" As the music ended, he took her arm and guided her to the side of the room. It had been a long time since a pretty ingénue had amused him so much. "Perhaps," he murmured, "yes, perhaps I *shall* seduce you."

She shook her head. "No, sir, you shall not."

"Oho, a challenge, my lady?"

"Not at all. 'Tis merely that I have no wish to be seduced." She held out her hand. "Thank you for the dance, my lord," she said dismissively.

He bowed, brushing her fingers with his lips. "Then I must make you fall in love with me."

Sarah frowned, her serious green eyes meeting his. "I would rather you did not make the attempt, sir."

For a long moment they stared at one another. The earl was intrigued by this absurd young woman—a country nobody who dared to defy one of the richest men in England.

"Madam, this is my dance, I think." Sir Thomas' words broke the spell.

Sarah turned to her husband, smiling. "Indeed, dear sir, I had begun to fear you had abandoned me. My lord." Another small curtsey to the earl. "Thank you for your company. If you will excuse me..."

Lord Cordeaux watched the couple walk away, until a soft voice spoke at his shoulder.

"How now, my lord—do I have a rival?"

The lime green brocade brushed at his legs.

"What's that. madam?"

"The little Methven—some sort of country cousin to Lady Marcham, I believe." The lady tittered. "Hardly your style, Cordeaux."

He stared at her for a long moment, as though he did not understand her words. Then he smiled.

"No, madam. Not my style at all."

Chapter Four

Jez sat on the bed and looked around her. The hotel room was enormous—as big as the whole ground floor of Lilac Cottage. As well as the big four-poster double bed and vast wardrobe, there was a beautiful walnut writing desk against one wall and a huge squashy sofa in the bay window. Dark oak panelling covered the lower half of the walls, the remainder being papered in a creamy silk, which contrasted with the rich red of the heavy brocade curtains around the bed and at the windows. A small refrigerator stood in one corner and she walked over to it, opening her eyes wide at the prices printed on the tariff sheet resting on the top. She unpacked her case and was running a bath when the telephone rang. It was Piers.

"Jessica? Look, my meeting's been cancelled—the guy can't get here until tomorrow, so I'll meet you for dinner, eight thirty."

Jez bit her lip. No invitation, just a cool assumption that she would be there. She glanced at her watch. It was only seven o'clock, but she had eaten virtually nothing at lunchtime and now she was starving.

"Could we make it earlier? I wanted to get an early night..."

She could almost hear his exasperation through the receiver.

"Okay. See you in the lounge at eight."

Jez grinned to herself as she slipped into the bath. He was

obviously used to making all the decisions, but why should she fall in with his plans? The worst he could do was sack her.

She was ready early but reluctant to leave her room. She decided to ring Harry and when there was no reply, she tried Kate's number.

"Hi! Guess where I am. The Manor—it's a really plush place somewhere south of Birmingham... Really expensive, bathrobes, slippers, sound system in the room, the lot. I've even got a four-poster bed. And guess who's in the same hotel...Piers Cordeaux."

"You mean the rich guy who asked you out? Good for you."

Jez laughed. "It's not like that! It's just that the other hotel was full, and this was the only place they could fit me in—"

"I've heard that before!"

"It's true, Kate. Not that I'm objecting, it's a fabulous place."

"Well, enjoy it and don't do anything I wouldn't do—which gives you quite a bit of scope."

"Thanks! Must go—time for dinner." Jez put the phone down, grinning. She was going to take Kate's advice and enjoy herself.

The lounge was a large, welcoming room full of big comfortable sofas. A blazing log fire burned in the hearth beneath the ornately carved chimneypiece. Jez walked in to find Piers waiting for her. He rose as she approached, and she did not fail to notice the envious glances thrown at her from the other women in the room. This did not surprise her—Piers was by far the most attractive man there. Taking in his casual navy shirt and chinos, Jez was glad she had chosen a white silk shirt worn loose over tight black trousers—and the high boots that

Harry said made her legs go on forever. Maybe she could have put up her hair, but in strange surroundings she liked to have the red-gold curls loose around her shoulders; they provided a convenient curtain for her face if she felt shy or embarrassed. However, tonight she knew she looked good, and that boosted her confidence, even in the face of her companion's perfunctory greeting. She tried to be charitable; Piers could be tired.

"Would you like a drink?" He signalled to a waiter.

"Thank you. Mineral water."

They sat down on either side of the fire, facing each other across the coffee table.

"Do you always stay here?"

"Yes. It's very convenient. I also like to keep it in the family." He noted her puzzled frown and pointed to the elaborate stone carving on the chimneypiece. "That's the Cordeaux family crest. This place was built as a hunting lodge by one of my ancestors. At one time we owned a large area of Warwickshire and Leicestershire."

"Really?" She looked up at the carving, a quartered shield with heraldic beasts she did not recognise, but there was one creature she could not mistake. "Does the sheep denote any family traits?"

He showed his teeth. "No, it's where our fortune came from. The Cordeaux males have more often been described as wolves."

She let that pass. "And can you always get a room here? Is it never fully booked?"

"Not to me."

She could imagine the management hastily rearranging their bookings to accommodate the rich Piers Cordeaux.

A waiter appeared and handed them the leather-bound menus. Another followed with their drinks then withdrew, leaving them to decide upon their meal. The menu was extensive and thankfully in English. Jez had to steel herself to ignore the prices—the starters alone cost more than she spent on a whole meal for Harry and herself. No wonder the sales team had looked at her enviously when they heard she was staying here. Well, she would make the most of it. When the waiter returned she chose a simple salad to begin her meal.

"And for the main course, madam?" The waiter hovered solicitously.

"I'll have the turbot." She had never eaten turbot, but she guessed it wouldn't taste that different from any other fish.

Piers nodded. "I'll have the same."

As the waiter moved off, his place was taken by a second white-coated young man.

"Would you like to order wine, sir?"

He had handed copies of the wine list to both Jez and Piers, but she noticed that he expected the order from her companion, and hovered obsequiously at his elbow.

"The Mersault. Premier Cru."

She scanned the lists until she found it, and she choked at the price.

Piers looked up. "Did you say something?"

She swallowed. "Yes. Actually, I'd like the house wine. Semillon blanc is very good with fish." *And this one's a quarter of the price*, she added silently.

The wine waiter glared at her, then looked back at Piers, who shrugged.

"Fine. We'll have that."

"As you wish, sir." The waiter nodded and moved off, his bearing expressive of disapproval.

"I think he's offended," observed Piers.

43

"He'll get over it. Perhaps he gets paid commission on the bill."

"Perhaps. Did you order the house wine because he ignored you?"

"No, I really like it. Although I have to confess I didn't like his servile attitude towards you."

"Was he servile? I didn't notice."

She gave him a kindly smile. "No, you wouldn't. You're used to it."

Jez watched the staff moving unobtrusively between the guests, taking orders, serving drinks and filling glasses. To be fair, they treated all their guests with equal courtesy, no extra distinguishing service for Piers, and if the maître d' himself summoned them to the dining room, she could not read too much into that.

The meal was excellent, and any misgivings Jez had about spending the evening alone with Piers Cordeaux soon evaporated. He was the perfect host and she found herself chatting away quite comfortably.

"Did you say your partner is an engineer?"

"Harry? Yes, with Tarrant International. Do you know them?"

"I've heard of them."

"They're one of the largest engineering companies in Europe. Harry's very lucky to be working for them."

"Harry...what? Have you been together long?"

"Gillam, Harry Gillam. We've been together for about eighteen months, but we've known each other for years."

She paused when the wine waiter appeared. Piers put his hand over his glass. He glanced across the table at her, his dark eyes glinting.

"No, no. This is the lady's choice. She should try it."

The waiter poured a little wine into the glass and Jez dutifully sipped it before nodding her approval. When the waiter had filled their glasses and moved away, she waited anxiously for Piers to try the wine.

"You're right," he said at last. "It is good."

Jez heaved a sigh of relief. "I thought I might be in trouble for a moment."

"Oh? Did you think I wouldn't like it?"

She observed the mischievous twinkle in his eyes and could not resist an answering grin.

"Well, actually, I don't know that much about wines," she confessed. "I could have made a *big* mistake."

"Well you didn't, so stop worrying."

His smile sent her heart rate soaring.

Whoa, girl, thought Jez, alarmed. *This is purely a business dinner, remember?* She struggled to think of a businesslike reply.

"At least your accountant will be pleased with me."

He shrugged. "It's covered by the marketing budget."

"But that's no reason to squander your money."

"Little puritan." He raised his brows. "Now what's the matter? Have I said something wrong?"

"No-o, just a case of *déjà vu*—you know, when you think you've said or heard something before and you know you haven't." She shivered. "I just had a strange feeling that I—I've done this before, which of course is rubbish. Spooky!" She laughed. "Perhaps it's the wine, some kind of retribution for choosing cheap plonk."

He smiled and raised his glass to her. "It certainly isn't

45

that. Let's forget it, and tell me instead if you like your fish."

"It's beautiful, and it beats cooking."

"What would you be doing if you were at home this evening?"

She looked at her watch. "Working. I have a job as a waitress two evenings a week at The Spinning Wheel. It's a local restaurant. It helps me pay my way. It wouldn't be fair for Harry to pay for everything while I'm studying."

"I thought your mother owned the cottage?"

She frowned. "How do you know that?"

"You told me."

"Did I? Yes, well, it was left to her. It's been in our family for generations."

"So do you and Harry have to pay rent?"

"No, but there are running expenses, and things like food, and my car, which is always breaking down."

"You're very defensive."

"Sorry—money's a bit of a sore subject when you haven't any."

"And I wouldn't know anything about that, of course."

The wine was making her brave. She met his eyes, a challenge in her own. "Well, do you?"

"As a matter of fact, yes. I left university with a few good ideas but no money. My parents had split when I was very young—my father went off God knows where and Mother had no funds, only the house. The banks weren't interested, so when Mother died and the house passed to me I sold everything and invested it in my first electronics company." He paused, studying the wine as he turned the glass between his long fingers. "Then I married the chairman's daughter and the rest, as they say, is history."

"It didn't work out?"

"She wanted bright lights and high living. I wanted to build another company. So we split. She's happy now, though. She married a shipping tycoon who dotes on her."

"I'm sorry."

"No need. It was a very long time ago."

"But I hate to think of any relationship failing."

He laughed and finished his wine. "Nothing lasts forever."

Jez could think of no reply, and she was grateful that the waiter came at that moment to clear away their dishes. She had not missed the note of bitterness in his voice, or the defensive gestures of one who did not want an old wound to be touched.

"Would you like dessert, sir—madam?"

Piers lifted a brow at her and Jez grinned.

"Oh you bet!"

"I thought you wanted an early night?" Piers looked at his watch. "It's after midnight."

Jez stared at him. "It can't be! It's gone so fast. I'm sorry—I've been prattling away at you all night. You must be bored to tears."

"Not in the least. Do you want a nightcap?"

She shook her head. "Thanks, but no. I won't be able to get up in the morning if I have anything else to drink. I just hope I don't get nightmares, the amount I've had to eat tonight. But it was delicious. Thank you, Piers."

As he led her through the darkly panelled corridors, she remarked, "I'm glad you're with me. I would never find my way through such a rabbit warren."

"Oh it's not so difficult once you've been here a few times.

This is your room, I think. Here, let me." He took her key and leaned past her to unlock the door.

Jez held her breath. He was so close she could detect a hint of spicy after-shave. She knew that if she leaned forward just an inch she could kiss his lean, dark cheek. Oh God, what was she thinking of! She quickly suppressed the thought and forced her lips into a smile. "Thank you."

"If I don't see you at breakfast, we'll meet in the lobby at eight thirty."

"Fine. Goodnight, Piers."

"Night. Sleep well."

He strolled away and Jez stepped into her room and closed the door, suddenly feeling very lonely.

"Oh snap out of it, girl!" she told herself crossly. "You're just disappointed that he didn't try anything. And why should he, when you've already told him you're not interested?"

She glanced at her watch: nearly one o'clock. Far too late to ring Harry now. She looked at the big four-poster bed, hung with red silks. Well, she would ring him in the morning and tell him just what luxury she was living in. She threw on her satin night-dress and slipped between the cool sheets, sinking back into the thick feather pillows. Sheer bliss!

Jez stretched luxuriously. This was a life she could get used to, she thought sleepily. A lady of leisure.

Chapter Five

Vauxhall Gardens blazed with light from the thousands of coloured lamps strung between the colonnades and the trees. It was the end of an exceptionally warm spring day, and the *beau monde* had flocked to the gardens where they rubbed shoulders with the lower orders as they strolled amongst the paths and avenues.

Sarah gave a gasp of delight and Her Grace the Duchess of Almondsbury glanced down at her, smiling.

"I am so glad Sir Thomas could spare you to me, Lady Methven. It is so amusing to introduce someone new to Vauxhall. I can enjoy the spectacle as if I, too, were seeing it all for the first time."

"It is magical," breathed Sarah, gazing about her through the slits of her mask. "I have never seen its like. Thank you for inviting me, madam, and also for the loan of this beautiful domino—I have never been to a masquerade before." She fingered the dark velvet cloak that enveloped her. She said shyly, "It is very kind of Your Grace to take such an interest in me."

"Indeed it is, Lady Methven, for I rarely bestir myself for others," came the frank reply. "But I cannot be untruthful to you, my dear. I did it for a dear friend of mine—a gentleman, who expressly wished you to be here tonight."

"I—I don't understand..."

"My Lord Cordeaux dropped me the hint, you innocent little puss, so what could I do but oblige him and bring you with me? Now, now, child, do not colour up so. I shall be perfectly discreet, I assure you!"

"No, no—that is, madam, you misunderstand," cried Sarah, distressed, but the Duchess had already turned away from her and was laughing with the other members of her party.

Short of leaving the group and making her own way home, Sarah had no choice but to accompany the duchess and her friends to the box that had been reserved for them for supper. The orchestra was already playing in the clearing a short distance away, and despite her misgivings, Sarah found the atmosphere of the gardens exhilarating. Surely, she thought, no harm could come to her in such a public place, and amongst such august company. The earl wished to see her. She could not but be flattered, and if he should go beyond the bounds of propriety, it would be up to her to bring him to his senses.

Sipping at the rack-punch served by a deferential liveried servant, she began to feel more cheerful. When at length the earl arrived she greeted him with her usual calm good manners, and if her fingers trembled a little when he raised them to his lips, surely he would make allowances for a little nervousness.

"Lady Methven." He pulled a chair beside her own. "I was afraid you would not come."

"I am here to see the gardens, sir," she said pointedly.

He laughed softly. "Do not toy with me, madam. Tell me you came to see me!"

She turned her serious gaze upon him. "Indeed, sir, I had no idea that you would be here, until her Grace mentioned it a moment since."

"Egad, madam, is that so?"

"Yes, my lord, it *is* so."

"But you are pleased to see me here."

"No sir."

He laughed. "By heaven, madam, you are very forthright."

"If I am sir, it is because you are impervious to anything less."

"Why do you imagine I am here, Sarah Methven?"

"To flirt with me," came the prompt reply. "You try to make such game of me every time we meet, my lord, and I would have you believe me when I tell you I do not want that."

"Make game of you! Since you came to London I have only seen you at balls and routs in the company of your husband, and we scarcely exchange a dozen words before you are whisked away from me. I confess I want you all to myself, just once, so that we can talk undisturbed for more than a few moments. Let us call a truce. Can we not spend the evening together—as friends?"

She looked at him suspiciously, but he merely raised his brows and returned her gaze innocently.

"You want to *talk* to me?"

"Of course. I want to know all about you. Tell me of your family."

"My father is the vicar of Burford." She added, lest he should doubt her breeding, "A gentleman's son."

"I did not doubt it. The church is a very honourable calling."

"Papa works so hard for his parishioners—and Mama too. She is his constant companion and helper. There is a truly Christian spirit between them. No-one is ever turned from their door."

"And when did you marry?"

"Four years ago. We live but three miles from my parents—a very suitable arrangement."

"And your husband? Tell me of him."

"Thomas is a good man. He works very diligently on the estate. Of course, he did not expect to inherit the baronetcy." She smiled, forgetting her resolution to remain aloof. "Poor Thomas, he would prefer to be riding out over the Home Farm, not escorting me to balls and parties, but he thought it his duty to bring me to Town, just once." She stopped, suddenly uncomfortable with the subject. "You have heard enough of me, my lord—tell me of yourself."

The earl selected a sweetmeat from the dish on the table beside them. "Me? I am as you see me, madam. Rich as Croesus and devoted to pleasure. I married my countess ten years ago and we live very happily—apart."

"Married!" Sarah's eyes flew to his face. "Oh, but—from what you have said to me..."

"What a little innocent you are. Our marriage was arranged when we were both in the cradle. Margaret has done her duty by providing me with an heir, and now we prefer to lead our separate lives. She lives in a neat little property of mine near Bath, where she enjoys the freedom accorded only to married women of rank, but unhindered by the presence of a husband. Why do you look at me so? What have I said to distress you?"

"I am sorry, it is none of my concern but—oh, I pity you, sir!"

He stared at her, his lip curling. "What's this? Little Sarah Methven, poor country miss—you pity *me*?"

She hung her head. "You are offended."

"Not at all, but I think you mistake, madam. I am the Earl of Cordeaux, one of the richest men in the country. No door is closed to me, there is nothing I cannot obtain."

"For all that, I cannot believe you are happy."

His blue eyes searched her face. She returned his gaze steadily. Suddenly a wry smile twisted his lips.

"You are in earnest." He picked up her hand and kissed it. "Oh Sarah, you enchant me."

"I do not mean to do so, my lord," she said, pulling her hand away.

"Little Puritan! That is one of your greatest charms." He refilled her glass. "If—*if* I promise not to importune you—would you walk with me, Sarah?"

"I would rather not sir."

"What, afraid?"

A faint blush tinged her unpowdered cheek.

"Not of you, my lord," she said, incurably honest.

"But this could be your only visit here and you have not seen the half of it—there's the fountains and the statuary...oh, a host of little delights."

"I confess I *should* like to see them, and I doubt Thomas would bring me again..."

The earl rose and from the corner of the box the Duchess of Almondsbury cast him a knowing glance. She was about to speak but he quelled her with a look. He held out his hand.

"Lady Methven, pray allow me to escort you through the gardens."

"You promise not to—to flirt with me?"

"You have my word on it."

With a sudden smile she gave him her hand and stepped out of the box on his arm.

Watching their departure, the Duchess nodded to her friends.

"Trusting little soul—like a lamb to the slaughter."

Chapter Six

The earl guided his partner through the lighted avenues, directing her attention to the pretty little lakes and ingenious grottoes that lined their route. Sarah suspected that he had walked this way many times before, but it did not dampen her own pleasure. The crowds jostled around them, and she was grateful for the anonymity provided by the domino and mask and also for the earl's tall and reassuring presence. It made no sense to her, but while he was beside her she felt secure, protected from the rougher, rowdy elements that milled about them. She allowed him to lead her along a little-used path, so closely edged by trees that their branches met overhead to form a tunnel. She looked up at the gaily coloured lanterns that lit the way.

"Oh, it is like a fairy-tale. I have no doubt it seems very commonplace to you, my lord, for you may visit it whenever you choose, but I have never seen its like before." She smiled up at him, her green eyes glittering through the slits of her mask.

Lord Cordeaux caught his breath.

"By Heaven, Sarah, I would like to give you emeralds to match your eyes."

She laughed.

"Very prettily said, sir, but I beg you will do no such thing. It would be most improper."

He stopped and put a finger under her chin, tilting her face up so that she was obliged to look at him. She met his look with a smiling, innocent gaze and he was aware of desire stirring within him.

"But I want to be improper." He kissed her gently. Then, when she did not resist him, he caught her in his arms, his lips on hers, hungrily demanding a response. He felt her flutter in his arms, like a bird with no power to resist him, then her hands were pushing against his chest.

"No—oh, my lord, I beg you, no more!"

He loosened his hold, but to his surprise she did not spring away from him in a fury of indignation, but clung to his coat, burying her face in the snowy lace that frothed above his waistcoat.

"Oh, sir. Forgive me!"

"What in heaven—! My dear child, I was the one who kissed *you.* Why do you not berate *me*?"

"I should never have come here. My lord—"

"I have a name, my dear. Will you not call me Richard?"

Again the emerald eyes were turned towards him, their colour deepened by her tears.

"I cannot call you that."

"Yes you can."

She pulled out of his arms and turned away, removing her mask to wipe her eyes. "Oh, what have I done!"

"You did nothing to be ashamed of, my dear."

"Oh, but I have! Do you not see that if I had not walked here with you, if I had not come here tonight—"

"I would have found some other way to get you alone. My dear, you have bewitched me."

"But I did not *want* to bewitch you. I never wanted that."

"Well, it has happened, and it is too late to turn back now."

"But we must. This cannot continue. It is a sin."

"My dear girl, it is the most common thing in the world. Young married women come to town with their dull, respectable husbands, they enjoy a few weeks' dalliance and return to the country to take up their dull, respectable lives, happy to have tasted a little pleasure. What is so wrong in that?"

She pushed him away and stared up at him in horror. "You think that I—that I would—"

"No, no, not you. I have known since I first met you that you were something different—"

She put her hands to her cheeks. "Oh I am undone! I must go—will you find me a carriage, sir—and make my excuses to The Duchess? Tell her I have the headache."

"You need not worry yourself over her Grace, she will not be expecting you to return to her this evening."

She stared at him, aghast. "You mean she thinks I am—that you—oh Heavens!"

She picked up her skirts and turned, hurrying back along the paths. With a muttered oath the earl followed, lengthening his stride to match her pace.

"Now where are you going?"

"I am leaving."

"Then my dear child, you are going the wrong way."

Sarah stopped. She looked about her wildly, unsure which route to take. The earl caught her arm.

"You are in earnest." He sighed. "Very well, if you really wish to leave, Sarah, let me escort you."

For a moment she hesitated. The crowds swirled about her

in a noisy confusion. She would never find her way out of the gardens alone. Then there were the ferrymen, rough, loud-voiced individuals who would look askance at a woman travelling alone, without even a maid to accompany her. Her courage failed.

"Thank you. I would be grateful for that."

The earl proffered his arm, and after the briefest hesitation she laid her fingers on his sleeve. As he guided her out of the gardens he reflected that he could as easily take her to one of the shadowed arbours and seduce her. She had responded to his kiss, before her strict morals got in the way. Perhaps he should take her now to some darkened bower where he would kiss her again, and go on kissing her until she gave in to the passion he knew was in her. He looked down at her, gliding along beside him, looking neither right nor left as they hurried through the dark walks. Adorable little prude, he would have her, but not by force. She must come to him willingly, and she would, he was sure. All he needed was a little patience.

When they reached the main gates, a word from the earl sent a lackey running to summon his coach. Minutes later and he was handing Sarah into the velvety darkness of the carriage.

As the coach pulled away, the earl found her hand and squeezed it.

"Lady Methven, my behaviour has distressed you. I apologise—"

"Sir, it is my own behaviour that has overset me! That I should fall to temptation so readily."

In the darkness she saw the white flash of his teeth as he grinned at her.

"'Tis easily done, madam—I fall constantly." A sob escaped her and he was immediately contrite. "Ah love, don't cry," he begged, taking her in his arms. "I would not see you unhappy."

Finding his shoulder conveniently close, she rested her head against him. He laid his cheek against her hair, and she could smell the spicy scent of sandalwood as his arms tightened around her. It was the most natural thing in the world for her to lift her face to his, inviting his kiss, and he obliged her with such tenderness that her objections melted away. She clung to him, for the first time in her life experiencing real pleasure in a man's embrace. She was gripped by a heady excitement. Tentatively she responded to his kiss, and when he tried to break away she pulled him to her once again. He laughed softly at her eagerness.

"*Doucement*, little one. Let me catch my breath." He shifted his position and lifted her onto his knees. She lay back against his arm, staring up into his eyes, which seemed to glow in the near-darkness. His head swooped down and he kissed her again. She put a hand to his cheek and felt his own fingers moving over her breast, causing such a fire to course through her that she moaned with pleasure.

"Let me direct the coachman to Kensington. I can still have you home before dawn."

His words sent a shiver of excitement through her, then she realised their meaning and a cold chill ran down her spine. She must stop this now, while there was still time. With a sob she pushed away from him and moved to the far corner of the carriage. She found that she was shaking.

"My lord, I will not. You must take me directly to Lady Marcham."

There was a long silence.

"As you wish, madam."

She peered through the gloom, trying to read his expression. "You will?"

"The coachman has his orders already, Lady Methven."

"Oh."

The coach rumbled on through the darkness. Sarah could still feel the excitement within her, the desire to throw herself back into his arms.

At last she could bear the silence no longer. "I have behaved most reprehensibly. I would be obliged sir if you could forget everything that has occurred this evening."

"In that, madam, I cannot obey you—I have enjoyed it too much."

Her cheeks grew warm. "Oh! Oh, that is so pretty! But my lord, you must not say such things to me. I am married."

"What has that to say to anything?"

She clasped her hands tightly in her lap, digging her nails into the palms to quell the feelings of desire. "I made my vows to my husband before God. I will not break them, and I beg you not to ask it of me."

"Do you deny you want me?"

"No, sir," she whispered. "I have never wanted anyone more."

"Then come with me."

"No, sir."

His teeth gleamed through the darkness as he grinned.

"I will have you, Sarah Methven. You cannot fight me."

"Oh my lord," she said desperately. "I must!"

When they reached Lady Marcham's townhouse, Sarah alighted alone and was admitted to the house by a sleepy lackey who had been ordered to wait up for her. The house was silent, even her husband had retired and Sarah could only be thankful. Her disordered spirits would not endure scrutiny.

Chapter Seven

"Miss Skelton? This is your morning call, compliments of the Manor Hotel. It's seven o'clock..."

"Yes, yes, thank you." Jez replaced the receiver and fumbled for the light switch, then she lay back on the pillows with a groan. She did not feel at all rested. She couldn't remember dreaming, but a vague unease disturbed her. She looked at the room. The dark panelling that had seemed so cosy and welcoming the night before now looked distinctly gloomy. With sudden decision she climbed out of the huge bed and went around the room, systematically turning on every light. That was better. Now all she needed was breakfast and she'd be ready to face the day.

Piers was already at breakfast when Jez entered the dining room. He looked up smiling as she joined him. She remembered Melanie's words—*wait 'til he gives you that come-to-bed look.* With a mental shake she reminded herself that she had only just got up.

"Good morning. Did you sleep well?"

"Yes—no—actually, I can't remember anything, so I *must* have done, but I think that huge meal last night made me restless. But please don't think I'm complaining, I had a great time."

"Good. So did I."

"I'm also very glad I didn't have to eat here alone on my first night. I'm sorry, though, that your business dinner didn't come off. Was he an important contact?"

"He could be. Unfortunately, he's off to the Far East tomorrow, but we've arranged to meet up this evening. There's a DTI reception tonight, to mark the end of the exhibition and he's going to be there." He paused. "Why don't you come with me?"

"Me! B-but why?"

"Why not? I'll arrange a ticket for you. You might find it interesting."

"Yes, I'm sure I would, but—I've nothing to wear!"

He laughed. "That's not very original."

"No, but it's true! I didn't come prepared for any dressy events."

"Well, if that's your only objection, there's no problem." He pushed aside his plate and rose. "I'll see you in the lobby in half-hour."

It was a clear, crisp October morning, with the trees decked in the golden yellows and reds of autumn. Jez filled her lungs with the cool air as they walked out of the hotel and across the drive to the car. The uneasiness of her restless night had worn off, and the bright sunshine made her feel glad to be alive. As they drove away from the hotel Piers asked her if she had found time to phone home.

"How's Harry coping without you?"

"He's managing very well."

"But he's missing you?"

"Yes, I suppose so. I didn't ask. How long does it take to get to the NEC?"

"We're taking a little detour first."

"Oh?"

"Mm. We have to buy you a uniform."

"You must be joking!"

"No, no. As part of CME, even temporarily, there are times when you will be representing the company and you will need a uniform."

"What sort of uniform?" she asked, suspicious, but Piers would only smile and shake his head.

She thought of the businesslike woollen suit that she was wearing under her thick coat—wasn't it good enough? Her mind buzzed with questions, but she knew it would be useless to ask them, so she maintained what she hoped was a dignified silence which lasted until they reached the motorway and headed south.

"So where are we going?"

"Cheltenham."

"Cheltenham! But—but why?"

"That's where we'll get your uniform. Don't worry about the exhibition. I've told the team we'll be late."

Jez sat in stunned silence as the car sped south. Her thoughts raced. She could not begin to understand, but he was the boss, so there was nothing to do but go along with it.

It took almost an hour to reach Cheltenham, and at last Piers pulled in to a wide road flanked with Regency townhouses. Bemused, she followed him out of the car.

"Come on. This is it."

He headed for a small shop. "Simone" was written in large gold letters above the window, which was dressed in nothing more than a dramatic arrangement of dried and gilded plants. Inside, the narrow shop held racks of ladies' suits and dresses, and an elegant curving staircase led to upper and lower floors. Jez wondered if the work-wear would be upstairs, or in the basement. The first surprise was the lady who appeared from between the racks of suits.

"Piers, darling! Such a long time." She came forward, her hands held out in greeting and her cheek turned up to receive his kiss. She was tall and slim, with the graceful elegance of a dancer. Her pale hair was swept back from a face that was still beautiful, although Jez guessed she must be at least sixty.

"Hello Maggie. How are you?"

"Very well, my dear boy, except that you do not come to see me enough. Now, who is this you have brought with you?"

"Maggie, this is Jessica Skelton. She's working with my company for a while and needs a dress for tonight. Something suitable for a business reception."

Jez stared at Piers, surprise and indignation robbing her of words while the older woman ran an expert eye over her.

"Size twelve, I'd say, and a gorgeous figure—like all your women, Piers."

"I'm sorry, but I am *not* one of his women!" Jez found she was almost grinding her teeth in fury.

"No, of course not, what a silly mistake." Maggie smiled. "Come upstairs and we'll see what we have in your size."

"I thought you said a uniform!" Jez hissed as they followed Maggie upstairs.

He grinned. "So it is. If we're going to an official function, you have to look the part."

She stopped on the stairs and turned. "Oh, and just what part is that?" she asked in a dangerous voice.

"My, er, assistant."

"Huh! Everyone will say I'm your latest conquest."

"Do you mind what everyone says?" The warm smile in his eyes never wavered from her face and she felt herself weakening.

"No, but I never said I'd come with you!"

"Oh? Have you something better to do tonight?"

"Come along, you two, there's work to be done." Maggie's voice saved her from having to answer him.

When she reached the first floor Jez stopped, blinking in surprise. The room was lined with row upon row of evening gowns ranging from full-skirted scarlet ball-gowns to slinky black silk dresses.

Maggie quickly moved along the lines, pulling out a dress here and there. "Now, what sort of reception is it?"

"Oh, the usual the sort of thing." Piers shrugged. "Cheap champagne, long speeches, tedious dinner and lots of prospective clients to impress."

Maggie pulled out an assortment of dresses from the racks while Piers lowered himself into a chair by the window.

"You'd better try them on."

Jez stood in the little cubicle and stared at her reflection in the mirror. After a succession of dark gowns Maggie had passed her a long dress in a pale cream. Its delicate lace pattern of crocheted silk lay like a dewy cobweb on an underdress of light coffee-coloured satin. She had to admit the dress was flattering. The strappy bodice hugged the natural curves of her body, and the colour enhanced the creamy tones of her skin. Maggie twitched back the curtain and handed her a pair of gold sandals with a slim heel.

"Try these with it."

Jez stepped out into the room and looked self-consciously towards Piers. She felt a quite childish pleasure in his look of admiration. Maggie was nodding approvingly.

"It's perfect for you, my dear, especially with that glorious hair. You can bet that most of the other women will be in black—very safe, but very boring. Do you like it?"

Jez looked at herself in the long mirror. "Oh yes. I love it, but—"

"We'll take it. Wrap it up for me, Maggie, and put it on the account."

"How much is it, please?" asked Jez.

Maggie smiled. "A lot, darling, but don't worry. Piers is picking up the tab."

"No." Jez shook her head. "No, I can't. I can't possibly have you buying dresses for me."

"Don't worry, I'm not going to make a habit of it, but I've already told you, I don't expect you to attend a company event without the right clothes."

"You make it sound so reasonable."

"It *is* reasonable. Now go and take it off so that Maggie can wrap up. The shoes too, and I'm sure we can find a suitable purse to go with it?"

Their late arrival at the exhibition stand did not go unnoticed. Jez observed Dave's raised eyebrows and Lavinia's frown but Piers gave them no time to ask questions.

"Sorry we're late: I had an appointment in Solihull—mainly company development but I thought Jessica might find it useful. Have we missed anything?"

"Couple of enquiries, nothing major," replied Lavinia. "You

know nothing happens much before lunchtime." She turned to Jessica. "So was your meeting interesting?"

Piers put up his hand.

"No point in asking Jez about it, Vinnie. Corporate information—I've sworn her to secrecy." His easy smile robbed the words of offence.

Jez blinked at his smooth explanation. You had to admire his technique.

"So you're not telling them about my uniform?" she murmured.

Piers' blue eyes glinted as he looked down at her. "No point in upsetting them, and just think of the speculation it would cause."

She *was* thinking of it. He was right, they would never understand, and she wasn't sure that she did. Remembering the boxes they had left in the Porsche gave her a tiny kick of excitement. It was like Christmas, only she couldn't tell anyone.

Jez tried to concentrate on the exhibition. She stayed in the background, watching Piers and the sales team talking to visitors, demonstrating the software, handing out demonstration discs and taking contact details. Lunch consisted of sandwiches discreetly consumed in the stand's cupboard-size office. Dave Kent paused for a word with her.

"Well, what do you think of it?"

"Fascinating. I just wish I could be more help."

"Don't worry. You're only here to observe. No-one expects you to sell the stuff."

"I know that, but I feel pretty awkward and, well, in the way."

"We all feel like that at times. Look, why don't you take a walk around the hall? Take a look at the other exhibitors. On the whole they're a friendly bunch, especially if you tell them you're a student."

"It would be useful, but—d'you think Vinnie would mind? After all, I am meant to be working with her."

"Vinnie would mind what?" The marketing manager came up, smiling. The day was going very well.

"I was suggesting Jessica should take a look at the other stands. Might pick up something useful."

"Sure. There's little for you to do here. Take your time."

"There you are, you have permission." Dave grinned. "Now go on. No need to rush back. Hopefully we'll all be busy here until five."

She did not see Piers again until they were ready to leave.

"So where were you all afternoon?"

"I went off to look at the other stands and talk to the competition. Lavinia said it was okay—I hope you don't mind."

"Not unless you told them all our secrets."

Her eyes flew to his face as she thought of their morning dash to Cheltenham.

"Industrial ones, that is," he added, his mouth quirking into a smile.

She relaxed again and grinned back at him.

"I don't know any! But, seriously, I picked up a lot of information on marketing and exhibitions—very useful for my report. I'll have to write up my notes tonight."

"You want to cry off from the reception?"

"After you bought me my—uniform? No way!"

Jez stood in the hotel lobby and surreptitiously studied

herself in one of the long mirrors that adorned the walls. She was quietly pleased with the effect. She had thrown her dark coat over her shoulders like a cloak and it fell open to reveal the beautiful cream dress. Her hair, freshly washed and pinned up, formed a red-gold frame for a face that looked unfamiliar. She had applied her makeup carefully but a little more freely than she did during the day, and the darker colours made her eyes look large and luminous in the soft lighting. She heard a low whistle and turned to find Piers behind her.

"Well, you'll certainly be an asset to the company in that!"

"Do you like it?"

"Very much. But you know what everyone will say."

She put up her chin. "Let them. I intend to enjoy myself."

Chapter Eight

Sitting in the huge banqueting hall listening to the third speech of the evening, Jez recalled Piers' words to Maggie that morning—cheap champagne, tedious dinner and long speeches. He had been right, although she had to take his word on the cost of the bubbly, which tasted fine to her. The dinner had been pleasant enough, but Piers had managed to secure a place next to his important business contact at dinner and they were soon deep in conversation. Jez found herself spending most of the meal listening to the red-faced businessman beside her. He had been drinking freely all evening and wanted to tell her in detail how he had single-handedly built up his import business, followed by a maudlin account of why his wife did not understand the long hours he spent in London. Now, as the speaker sat down to polite applause, Jez realised that Piers was standing up, shaking hands with his companion.

"Early plane to catch?" she asked as Piers lowered himself back into his seat.

"Yes, he has to leave at six. Sorry if I've been ignoring you—you probably wish you'd stayed at the hotel."

"Not at all," she lied brightly.

He looked at his watch. "Look, there'll be nothing going on here now, except more drinking. How about we get back to the Manor and have a nightcap?"

The red-faced man beside her touched her arm. "C'n I get you another drink, m'dear?"

Jez smiled and reached for her bag. "Thanks very much, but we're leaving now."

Piers collected her coat and escorted her to the main entrance, where a taxi appeared for them as if by magic. They spoke very little on the journey. Jez stole a glance at her companion. He looked tired. She realised suddenly just how hard he had been working, on the stand all day, keyed up, seeking new business, then an evening spent talking shop. While she had been free to enjoy her meal, he had been busy building a rapport with another potential customer. He caught her eye.

"Anything wrong?"

"You're never off-duty, are you?"

"I am now."

"Look, I'm really not bothered about that nightcap. If you'd rather give it a miss—"

"No, no, I'd like to, unless you are too tired..."

"No, I just thought—" She shrugged and smiled. "Fine."

The lounge of the Old Manor was quiet and welcoming after the smoky after-dinner atmosphere of the banqueting room. Jez chose her favourite spot on one of the sofas by the fire.

"Brandy, coffee or both?" Piers noticed her hesitation and added, "I'm having both."

"Then I'll have the same, thank you." She leaned back against the cushions and gave an exaggerated sigh. "This is heaven. So peaceful."

Piers settled himself on one end of the sofa and turned so that he could watch her, one arm resting along the back of the cushions and a faint smile in his dark eyes. "You wouldn't prefer to finish the evening clubbing in Birmingham?"

"No way. I'm not a party animal. I prefer a small gathering of friends, or even curling up at home with a good book. Very boring. But what about you, what do you do when you are not working?"

"When I can take a few weeks off I like to go sailing, or skiing. Do you sail?'

"No, but I've been skiing a couple of times." She sipped at her brandy and looked up to find Piers giving her an appraising glance. Was he thinking how good she would look in ski pants? The thought warmed her even more than the spirit in her glass.

"What about when you're in London?" she asked. "Where do you go?"

"I rarely go out in town, except for a meal with a few close friends, maybe."

"But there's so much going on in London! What about the theatre? You must have the best shows in the country. Just think of it, all those plays and new productions, not to mention the musicals. Then there's the ballet and opera—God, if I lived in London I'd want to go to something new at least once a week!"

"Not much fun on your own."

She laughed at him.

"Poor little rich boy! Don't tell me you can't find someone to go with you. You are always being photographed with some gorgeous blonde on your arm."

Hell, she shouldn't have said that, he would think she was jealous. She put down her glass. The brandy was making her reckless.

Piers merely shrugged. "Yes, but that's usually when I've

been invited to attend something as Chairman of CME, not plain old Piers Cordeaux. Besides, most of 'em don't actually like the arts much."

She said quietly, "It must be very lonely at the top."

"You get used to it. Now what's wrong—are you feeling sorry for me?"

Alarm bells were clamouring in her head. The conversation was getting dangerous. Jez sought frantically for a flippant response.

She opened her eyes wide. "What, impoverished Jez Skelton pitying the rich Mr. Cordeaux? Impossible!"

"I'm not so sure you're impressed by my money."

"I'm not. I'm more impressed that you are such a nice guy, despite your money and power. At least you don't flaunt your success in people's faces."

"Thank you."

"Sorry. That sounds like I'm creeping." She looked up to find him watching her, smiling. Her stomach lurched and dissolved within her. She looked away quickly from those disturbing deep blue eyes. "Is that the time? I'd better get some sleep if I'm going to be fit for anything tomorrow."

"I'll see you to your room."

The thick carpets deadened their footsteps in the empty corridors as they made their way through the old house. With Piers at her side, Jez's nerves were at full stretch. She wanted to take his hand, put her arm through his. To belong.

"Um—are we meeting up with Lavinia tomorrow? I'll need a lift back to Filchester."

"They will be having a sales briefing first at their hotel. Don't worry. I'll drive you home."

"Thank you."

They had reached her room but before Jez could speak again, Piers wished her good night and was walking away. She stepped inside and closed the door.

"Damn, damn, damn!" She threw her bag down in disgust. Here she was, dressed to kill and she had let him walk off without even a goodnight kiss. Perhaps he didn't fancy her—but that was not the point, she argued with herself. She knew she looked good in the cream dress, she had been aware of him looking at her several times during the evening. So why hadn't he tried anything?

Because you told him you're not available, came the obvious reply, but it did not satisfy her. She paced the room restlessly. "Oh this is stupid!" she said aloud. "Go run yourself a bath and forget it. You know very well you can't have him."

But she had never felt such a strong attraction before, not even for Harry when they had first started going out together. She perched on the edge of the bath, watching the hot water pour in. It was obviously a case of wanting what was not available. She reached for one of the complimentary packets of bath oil and poured it into the water. She might as well pamper herself.

As she was about to step into the bath, there was a soft knock at the door. Jez froze. Excitement swept through her. *Calm down,* she told herself sternly. *It's probably room service with the wrong number.* Probably.

Pulling on her robe, Jez opened the door cautiously. She was expecting to find Piers there but even so, when she saw him in the doorway, her heart gave a somersault. She fell back automatically, and he stepped into the room. He was still wearing his dinner jacket, but he had discarded the black tie.

He held up the bottle of champagne and glasses that he was carrying. "I thought this might just finish off the evening."

Jez's insides were mimicking the fizz of the champagne as she looked up at him. The glint in his eyes sent a shiver through her.

"I—um—I was just going to have a bath..."

His mouth curved into a slow grin.

"Then we can share that, too." He kicked the door shut. "Champagne now, or shall I put it in the minibar for later?"

She couldn't take her eyes from his face while her brain seemed to have stopped working. Piers was here, in her room. She watched, rooted to the spot, while he put down the champagne.

"I'm breaking my own rules here," he said, reaching for her.

"R-rules?"

"I never mix business with pleasure. At least, I haven't until now."

As he drew her towards him Jez felt a wave of joyous exultation. It was a heady mix of excitement, pleasure and, yes, lust. She lifted her head, her lips parting to receive his kiss. The touch of his lips shocked her. This was no gentle, exploratory caress: it was demanding, possessive, reaching to her very core. She gave herself up to him willingly, winding her arms around his neck and kissing him back with a passion she did not know she possessed. She stifled a moan of disappointment when he lifted his head. His hold did not slacken and he looked down at her, his eyes as black as coal. His breathing was as ragged as her own.

"Let's not rush it," he muttered. "I've waited a long time for this. I want to make it special." Almost reluctantly he put her away from him. "Finish running that bath. I'll join you in a moment."

The bubbles glistened diamond-bright in the gleaming white bath as Jez stepped in. Her body was still aroused and tingling from that kiss. The blood was singing in her veins—she had never felt so alive! With a little laugh she slid down into the water and let the sparkling bubbles envelope her body. She closed her eyes, shivering in anticipation of what was yet to come. Something, some slight sound, told her she was not alone. She opened her eyes to see Piers standing in the doorway. Her mouth dried at the sight of his strong, naked body, every muscle tanned and toned. She sat up as he handed her a glass of champagne.

"Wh-what are we celebrating?" Jez tried to speak lightly, but her voice croaked.

Piers lowered himself into the bath, his long legs sliding against hers.

"Finding each other." He lifted his glass to salute her.

Jez tingled with pleasure.

"Piers? What did you mean just now—you've waited a long time for this?"

He shrugged.

"The first time I saw you, trying to stop the runaway photocopier, I knew you were different, special."

She laughed.

"I bet you say that to all the girls."

"No. I don't think I've ever said it to anyone before."

She caught her breath when she looked into his eyes. The intensity of his look frightened her. It was gone in an instant and he was smiling again. He scooped up a handful of bubbles and smoothed them over her breast. "Not in the bath, anyway."

She gasped as his fingers caressed her nipple which hardened immediately. Piers laughed softly.

"Come on," he whispered. "I want to take you to bed."

As she climbed out of the bath he wrapped her in a soft, snowy bathsheet and lifted her into his arms. He carried her into the darkened bedroom to the four-poster bed where he laid her gently on the covers. She reached for him, wanting to pull him down to her but he shook his head.

"Not yet. I want to let your hair down."

Obligingly she knelt up on the bed while he pulled the pins from her hair until it fell like a heavy, shining curtain around her shoulders.

Piers stared at her. She met his gaze, a shy, tentative smile curving her lips. She was a dream come true. His heart soared at the sight of her white and gold beauty. Nervously she ran the tip of her tongue across her lips and his self-control snapped. He gently touched the soft white skin and felt her tremble beneath his fingers. With something between a sigh and a groan he reached for her, crushing her mouth beneath his. A rush of pleasure engulfed him when he realised she was responding, matching him kiss for kiss.

They fell together in a tangle of limbs, hands and feet stroking, caressing while they explored each other with mouths and fingers, touching, teasing, arousing one another until they were both gasping with delight and desire. His fingers trailed across her thighs, travelling over the soft flesh while she moved with his caresses, raising her hips, provocative, inviting. He entered her, heard her gasp beneath him, was momentarily aware of her fingers on his back, nails digging into the skin as she cried out his name, then everything was lost in a gasping, shuddering crescendo of pure, white-hot pleasure. It was as if he had come home.

§

It was still dark when Jez slipped out of bed. She pulled on her bathrobe and wrapped it about her to keep out the morning chill. Opening the curtains a little she could see only a grey mist. She reached for her glasses and the morning sky came into focus, the stars beginning to fade as the first grey lines of dawn appeared on the horizon.

"What have I done?"

She leaned against the window, pressing her forehead onto the cold glass as her mind wandered back. Piers sharing the bath with her—even now the thought of his lean, muscular body sent a pleasurable shudder of excitement through her. He had carried her to the bed, lifting her as easily as a child, and then he had made love to her. There were no other words to describe it; the excitement he had generated in her, and her own attempts to please him. She remembered getting out of bed to remove her contact lenses. The movement had disturbed Piers and when she had slipped back under the covers he took her in his arms and they had made love again. Everything had been so simple, so *right*. Even now she wanted to climb back into bed, to wrap herself around him and demand more—

"Jez?"

"I'm here."

"Come back to bed."

She fought back the tears.

"I can't." Turning, she sensed rather than saw Piers sitting up in the darkness.

"Jez? What's wrong?"

"Everything!" The words were wrenched out of her. In a moment Piers was beside her, cradling her in his arms as she cried.

"I'm sorry! I've let you down, and—and Harry—"

"Hush now, it's not as bad as all that. And we took

precautions..."

"That's not the problem!" She pushed him away. "H-Harry trusted me! I didn't even *think* of him, not once! How could I—"

"Maybe you just found me irresistible." His lips brushed her neck.

"Don't joke, Piers. I should never have allowed this to happen." He did not reply, and she sighed. "I'm going to shower."

When she came out of the bathroom, Piers was dressed and had made tea.

"Here, drink this."

"There's no milk."

"It's Earl Grey. Best way to drink it."

Jez took a sip and was pleasantly surprised.

"It's good. Thank you." She looked up at him and was again aware of that strong attraction. "What time do you want to get away?"

"There's no hurry. About ten."

"Piers—I'm sorry—"

He took the cup from her and pulled her into his arms. "I'm not. Would it help if I told you it was the best night I've had for a very long time?"

She felt the tears welling up again and she buried her head in his shoulder. "No. I feel such a dreadful, two-timing bitch!"

"Will you tell him?"

"I don't know."

"I think you should. I want to see you again, Jez."

She pulled away from him and went in search of a tissue.

"No, Piers. I'm not naïve enough to think this could be anything more than a one-night stand. We come from very

79

different worlds, you see. It would never work and we would only end up hurting ourselves and other people. It's better we stop it now."

There was a long, tense silence.

"All right, Jez. If that's what you want."

She could not look at him. "Yes."

His hand gripped her shoulder.

"I'll see you downstairs at ten."

When he had gone she stood for a long while, staring blankly at the painted wall. So that was it. Simple. He was gone, and the manner of his going, that hand on her shoulder with its final, comforting squeeze, it was like those old weepie romances she liked to watch, only this really hurt. She began to laugh hysterically until the laughter turned to tears and she threw herself on the bed, finding a measure of relief in crying.

Her anguished tears couldn't last, and finally she lay exhausted and silent. A faint movement of air seemed to sigh around the quiet room. Jez lay with her face buried in the pillow, her hair loose and heavy on her shoulders. She felt the gentle touch of a hand on her head and she angrily shook it off.

"Piers—I told you—go away!" She sat up, staring into emptiness.

There was no-one else in the room.

Chapter Nine

The journey back to Luxbury was not as bad as she had feared. Piers treated her with his usual friendly courtesy so that she began to lose her embarrassment. That was very necessary, she knew, if she was to stay at CME. Piers worked mainly from the London office, but it was impossible to believe that she could be there for another four or five months without seeing him at some point.

She took in the clean lines of his face, the strong determined jaw, decisive mouth, the dark, curling lashes fringing deep blue eyes that were now fixed on the road.

As if aware of her scrutiny, he flicked a look across at her. "What are you thinking?"

"Your watch." She tried for a lighter note.

"Pardon?"

"I was looking at your watch—is it a Rolex? I've never seen one before. What makes them so special, built-in video conferencing or something?"

"No, it just tells me the time. Status symbol," he added gravely. "You look a little pale. You sure you're all right?"

"Yes...Piers?" They were turning into the High Street.

"Look, if you're going to apologise again for last night, don't. It wasn't your fault—I'm not sure it was mine, either. Would you believe me if I said I didn't plan this to happen?"

"Huh! So you always carry condoms in your dinner jacket?"

His lips curled derisively.

"I keep some in my room at the hotel. I've had plenty of experience of women trying to slap a paternity suit on me!" He glanced at her, and his voice softened. "What I mean, Jez, is that I wasn't planning to make a move on you. I've always made it a personal rule not to get involved with my staff. Then I saw you last night in that dress, looking so damn gorgeous, and all my good intentions disappeared. You won't convince me that you didn't feel the same way, but I do understand your reasons for not wanting to take it further."

He pulled up at the cottage and climbed out of the car to open her door.

"You do?"

"Of course. Besides," he called after her as she was about to go inside, "you might change your mind yet."

She smiled, shaking her head, then, terrified she might start to cry, she whisked herself inside.

The following week was a nightmare for Jez. She had arrived at the cottage to find Harry suffering from a heavy cold and feeling very sorry for himself. She tucked him up in bed and kept him supplied with hot drinks, thankful to take on the role of ministering angel rather than resume that of lover.

Back in the office, it was soon apparent that everyone knew she had stayed at the Manor and they teased her, calling her Piers' girlfriend and asking her if he was any good in bed. They thought it a very good joke and Jez forced herself to respond in kind, knowing that she must give no hint at all that there was anything between herself and the head of the corporation. She only hoped that by the time he next put in an appearance at the

Filchester office, the joke would be forgotten.

Harry tottered between bed and the sofa for almost a week, and it was not until the following Thursday that he felt well enough to take himself off to work. Jez had not told him about Piers. He had been feeling far too unwell to ask about her trip, and she was too much of a coward to mention it.

However, as the days passed her conscience grew uncomfortably prickly, and she came home on the Thursday night determined to tell him everything. After all, there had never been any secrets between them. She rehearsed her speech all the way home in the car and walked into the house with the words almost bursting from her tongue. Harry was not there. She found a message from him on the answerphone to say that he would be late.

Jez could not help the sigh of relief that escaped her.

She decided not to waste the free time. Pulling out all her notes she began to plan her report. She had set herself a deadline of January for this section of her work, and there was a lot more to do to pull it all together.

As she was staring at the laptop screen she caught sight of a florist's van pulling up outside, but it was some minutes before she realised that the driver was bringing her a huge bouquet. With a cry of delight she lunged for the door to take the flowers from the startled deliveryman. She carried them carefully into the house, breathing in the faint perfume. Dear Harry, how thoughtful, and such a beautiful display of red and cream with leaves of glossy dark evergreen.

She pulled out the card and the smile died on her lips. There were just three words on the card, and a telephone number. *Ring me. Piers.* Arrogant man! She almost threw the bouquet down on the table, but the fragile beauty of the flowers was too beguiling and instead she took them to the kitchen to find a suitable container. She had no vases large enough for such a bouquet so in the end she split them, arranging the vivid red gerberas and the anemones in two vases and threading the long-stemmed tuberoses into a spaghetti jar with the evergreen leaves. The result made her grin—probably not the elegant display he had envisaged, but for all that they were beautiful.

She wouldn't ring him, of course, but she slid the card into her purse, just the same. The flowers settled it. She would have to tell Harry now.

Humming to herself, she took extra care over dinner and opened a bottle of wine, which she set on the table in the little dining room at the back of the house. The room was seldom used, for they preferred to have most of their meals on their knees in front of the television, but she decided that if she was going to tell Harry about Piers, she wanted his full attention.

The room felt cold and a damp, musty smell hung in the air. Jez lit a few scented candles and brought in a fan heater to augment the inadequate radiator. She heard the thud of the front door and called to Harry.

"Hi." He came in, still wrapped in his coat. "What are you doing in here?"

"I thought we might have dinner in here tonight."

He made a face. "I'd rather not, love, I've still got this wretched cold and all I want to do is put my feet up in front of the telly. Besides, I don't like this room. It's always so cold."

"Not tonight, though. I've brought in an extra heater—"

"I know, Jez, but that won't help much. The room's damp. Look, you can see where the paper's lifting down in that corner." He pulled gently at the edge of the wallpaper. "Shit! It's soaking wet. You'd better get someone to look at that, Jez. You could have dry rot, or something."

84

With that, Harry wandered away into the lounge, leaving Jez standing bemused in the dining room. A few moments later she heard the staccato sounds of the television as he flicked through the channels.

She stood in the doorway, glaring at the back of his fair head. "Do you like my flowers?"

"Mm? Oh." He glanced at the elegant tuberoses in the spaghetti jar. "Oh yes. Very nice. Treat yourself, did you?"

"No, they're from an admirer..." There was no reaction. "From a lover, as a matter of fact."

"Sorry love, what did you say?"

Jez bit her lip, trying not to feel ill-used. After all, Harry was not himself.

"Nothing. Dinner's nearly ready."

She went back into the dining room, cleared the table and prepared their meals on two trays. Perhaps she wouldn't tell him about Piers. Not tonight, anyway, and perhaps not ever. Mixed with her relief at this reprieve was an irritation at Harry's insensitivity. Could he not see that she had made an effort? *Piers would have noticed.* She pushed the thought away—*that* wasn't going to help. Guilt quickly succeeded the irritation. She knew she'd made the effort because she had been unfaithful and was trying to soften the blow.

Yet how typical of him to expect her to wait on him while he stretched out on the sofa and did nothing. And that was not all. She felt resentment welling up. She disliked the way that any problems with the house devolved to her. Okay, it was her house, or at least her mother's, but could he not share some of the maintenance, instead of leaving it all to her?

She mulled over these points during the evening, but Harry was oblivious to her silence. Later he strolled into the kitchen where she was washing up and he put his arms around her, nuzzling her ear.

"Sorry I haven't been much company tonight. This wretched cold has really taken it out of me."

Jez leaned back against him. "That's okay. Harry..."

"I think I'll get an early night. Got a busy day at work tomorrow." With a final squeeze he let her go and sauntered away. "Goodnight, love. See you in the morning."

Jez plunged her hands into the water.

"Damn him," she muttered. "Damn all men!"

Chapter Ten

"What you've got there is rising damp, see?"

Norman Jobbins from Luxbury Damp and Drainage Systems tapped his moisture meter with one stubby finger and nodded solemnly at Jez, who stared back at him in dismay. The man was short and broad with a red, weather-beaten face and wiry grey hairs growing out of his ears. "You're lucky though. It's only in this one wall, so all we need to do is knock off the plaster to about three foot, inject a chemical damp-proof course and re-plaster. That's the trouble with these old places, y'see, most of 'em were built directly onto the earth. No proper foundations. Course, we'll have to check your joists, take a few boards up, like."

Jez found her attention was wandering. Mr. Jobbins was wearing baggy cord trousers of a darkish green, very like the colour of lichen on a damp stone. She found herself wondering if he too had rising damp.

"—so when d'you want us to start?"

"Sorry?"

"I said you need this seein' to soon."

"How much will all this cost?"

"I'll price it all up and pop a quote in to you later this week."

"Would it be cheaper if *we* took off the old plaster?"

He rubbed a hand over his stubbly chin.

"Well, that would save you a bit, I s'pose... May I?" He eased away a piece of the paper. "You can see the damp line on the wall. You'll need to take the plaster off up to about here. Along the whole wall."

"Well then, that's what we'll do. You send me a quote for the rest of the work and I'll let you know when you can start."

Harry was less than keen when he heard Jez's plan.

"But it won't take us long to knock off the plaster," she explained. "Look, most of it is loose anyway. And don't forget it will keep the cost down—we have to decorate after, remember?"

"Yes, well, I'm getting busier at work, Jez, and I don't want to be working at home every evening."

"Okay, okay! I'll do it myself."

"Jez, don't be like that—" He caught at her hands. "I'm not saying I won't do it, just that it might take a bit longer. But then, there's no hurry, is there?"

They made love that night, the first time since Jez had returned from the exhibition. When it was over and Harry was asleep beside her, she lay in the darkness, tears of disappointment running silently over her cheeks.

"What's in the post this morning?" Harry came downstairs, running a hand through his hair.

"It's from Great Aunt Emmy." Jez read it avidly, then handed it to him. "You remember, Mum's auntie. Poor old thing's broken a bone in her foot and has to rest—hence the letter. Normally she can't sit still long enough to write to anyone. Poor Emmy, I'll give her a ring. Perhaps I can go and give her a hand this weekend. It must be very difficult for her."

"Do you want me to come with you? Only, I thought if I stayed here I could make a start on getting that plaster off..."

"Oh Harry, would you mind?"

He grinned. "Not at all, as a matter of fact I'd prefer it. I'm not very good at dealing with doddery old dears!"

Jez fought down her irritation at his way of referring to her favourite aunt. She smiled. "So that's what it takes to get you working. All right, you stay here, but there had better be some serious progress by the time I get back."

As she packed her bags for her weekend away, Jez realised how relieved she was to be going away on her own. *It will pass,* she told herself desperately. *We'll get back to normal if I just keep trying.*

§

Emilia Appleton lived in a large red-brick bungalow on the edge of Worcester. The building had little character externally, but inside it was crammed with antiques and possessions acquired over the years from various members of her family. A former librarian in Worcester, she had a love of the past that had now found its outlet in researching her family history. She was an energetic septuagenarian and a pillar of the local Women's Institute. When Jez had phoned to say she was coming over, Emmy had accepted her offer of help but had forbidden her to bring anything more than a bottle of wine.

As Jez drew up outside the house, her aunt threw open the door.

"Emmy, don't you dare come out here!" Jez climbed out of the car and grabbed her bags from the boot. "You stay there. I'll be with you in a second."

Once safely inside the house Jez returned her aunt's warm hug. "Oh, you poor old thing! What have you been doing to yourself?"

"Oh, it's nothing, just fell off a curbstone. But let me look at you...hmm...dark rings under your eyes, and you're as thin as a rake. You'd better come and tell me what's wrong."

"Nothing's wrong, Emmy. Now, let's get you sitting down. Didn't you say you'd promised the doctor to rest for most of the day?"

"Yes, well I have been sitting down until now."

"Then go and sit down again, and I'll put the kettle on. And I positively forbid you to touch any of my bags. I can put them all away while I'm waiting for the kettle to boil. Which room am I in, same as usual?"

Once she was sure that her aunt was resting in the little lounge, Jez took her bags through to the spare room. It held an old-fashioned bed, a large mahogany wardrobe, and a walnut chest of drawers with a serpentine front and a huge bowl of potpourri on top. Leaving her bags to be unpacked later, she went back to the kitchen to make tea.

She found her aunt had already prepared a salad supper for them, and after scolding her for being so busy, Jez set the meals on trays so that they could sit before the little gas fire in the lounge, where Emmy could keep her foot up on a stool.

"Oh, I am so glad you could come," said Emmy, smiling. "I was wondering what to do with myself this weekend. It's so boring being housebound."

"It must be hard for you to sit still for so long, Emmy. Usually you never stop. I've never known anyone with so much energy."

"But I'm not getting any younger, my dear. I am seventy-five, after all, and I can't go on forever."

Jez frowned. "Come on, Emmy, this maudlin mood isn't like you at all."

"No, but our mortality has been brought home to me recently. A couple of good friends have passed on and your great-great-aunt Caroline died a few months ago. You didn't really know her, did you? She's been in a nursing home for the past dozen years. Very frail, but then she was over ninety. Poor Caroline, she outlived all her own close family, and after she died her solicitor contacted me to tell me that she had left some family papers to me, as her nearest relative."

"Oh, that's great. Love letters?"

"Well, I've only glanced at a few of them so far. There's a few old photos, postcards and things, but the most interesting is a box of letters and a journal dating back to seventeen something."

"I'd love to have a look, if I may?"

"Of course. Can you get them, my dear? They are in a cardboard box, in the bottom of the wardrobe in your room."

Jez went out and returned moments later with a large box, which she put down on the floor before her aunt.

"Well, open it up, girl!"

Inside was a small mahogany box inlaid with an intricate marquetry design in harewood, ivory and brass.

"Oh, how lovely." Jessica slipped from her chair to kneel on the floor. She ran her fingers over the smooth wood. The hinges and clasp were of brass, and on the top there was a brass inlay entwining the letters *S* and *M*. Jessica looked up at her aunt.

"Sarah Methven, I think," said Emmy, "from what I've read so far."

"And is she a relative of ours?"

"Yes. At least, there is a Sarah in the family at about that time, but it's not a strand I've investigated. Her father was Patrick Appleton, the vicar of Burford. Her birth is recorded in the family bible. I looked it up—1723—but there's no other mention of her."

Jessica opened the box. It was lined with green silk, very thin and faded by time. Lying inside the box were bundles of folded, yellowed paper, each neatly tied with a green ribbon. "May I?"

"Of course. But be careful, they are very fragile. I am going to get them copied and then the originals can be stored properly. I've only glanced through them. It's mostly letters to Sarah Methven from her family, a letter from her mother, congratulations following the birth of her baby, that sort of thing. The names and places seem to tie up with the Appletons at that time, so I'm pretty sure she was Sarah Appleton before she married. There's even one very charred paper, looks as if it's been rescued from a fire. I haven't touched that, my love, because it's far too fragile, but I have a contact who might be able to help, if we think it's worth it."

Lying beneath the letters was a small leather-bound book. Jez lifted it out carefully.

"That's her journal," said Emmy. "It's faded and very difficult to read, but from the little I've managed to decipher there's nothing of any great historical significance there. It starts in 1746, with a visit to London, but then she only used it for a few months." She smiled indulgently. "I expect she was like all you young things, starting something then leaving it when the novelty wears off."

Jez opened the book and the pages crackled dangerously.

"'Sarah Methven.'" she read. "'Her journal, started this day of our Lord 15th April 1746. We are arrived in London at the home of Lady Marcham, Thomas' cousin...'" She looked up, her eyes shining. "Emmy, this is fantastic! We will be able to trace these names and dates, surely." She put down the journal and lifted out a bundle of letters, carefully untying the ribbon. Turning the faded writing to the light she frowned over the unfamiliar lettering. "Emmy, have you read these?"

"No love, I only looked at the first few, the writing is very scrawled and my eyes aren't as good as they were, you know."

"She's begging her husband to let her see her children. Listen, 'My dear Thomas. I must throw myself on your mercy, dear husband, and beg that you will read this letter and not return it unopened as you have done with my previous missives. My dear sir, I know that I have sinned most grievously, but having explained the circumstances of my behaviour, you must believe that I did not willingly abandon you and my darling little ones. Therefore I beg, sir, that you will allow me the opportunity to see little Thomas and my dear Jenny. I am their natural mother, and my heart cries out to know how my darlings go on. I implore you sir, to have some compassion for my plight. My behaviour was unpardonable, that I accept, and your refusal to take me back as your wife I can also understand, but that my children should be denied their mother's love is more than I can bear. Pray sir, allow me to see them. Yet, if your heart will not allow it, I beg you to send me some word of how they go on. I await your answer, sir, as your most humble servant and wife, Sarah.' What did she do, Emmy? Why was she kept away from her children?"

"I don't know dear, perhaps the answer will be in the other papers. We'll go through them in the morning, when the light is better. Don't puzzle your brain over it now. Let's put it all away for now, and I'll get us a nice bed-time drink. What would you like, brandy?"

"Please. Let me get them—"

"No, no, my love, I'm not an invalid, whatever the doctor may say."

Jez smiled to herself as her aunt went away to fetch two brandies. She knew from past experience they would be large measures. A stranger meeting Emilia Appleton for the first time might think she lived a quiet, genteel existence with meals on wheels and cocoa at bedtime, when in fact she was out to lunch most days and invariably drank a glass of scotch or brandy in the evenings. Jez hoped that she too would be as fit when she was seventy five.

At two o'clock in the morning Jez gave up the struggle and admitted that she was not going to sleep. She turned on the bedside lamp and lay for a few moments, listening. The bungalow was silent. She pulled on a sweater over her nightdress, picked up her glasses and went out to the kitchen to make herself a drink. The lounge door was open, and as she passed Jez glanced at the little mahogany box, still sitting on the coffee table. She made herself a cup of tea and went into the lounge. Kneeling before the little box she carefully opened the lid, took out the journal and began to read.

April 23rd, 1746

Dover Street

We have been in London for seven days and still I do not sleep for all the noise. It is so large, unlike home, and I miss the children, although Lady Marcham is most kind. Tomorrow we go to Court. I am to be presented! Who would believe that I, little Sally Methven the clergyman's daughter, would meet the King.

April 24ᵗʰ

Thomas and I took a carriage to St James's. I wore my new canary brocade with the embroidered petticoat. Lady M's own maid powered my hair and Thomas said I was the handsomest lady in the room! We were acknowledged by T's acquaintances, and the Earl was very kind to me, but T says he is a very wicked man and I must not acknowledge him.

April 29ᵗʰ

Tonight was Lady M's ball. She has given me a most beautiful figured silk that has been worked up to fit me. So many people, such noise—Lady M knows everyone of importance, whereas I know no-one. The Earl was here—Lady M introduced us, so how could I not talk to him? He dances very well and amused me with his nonsensical chatter. I cannot think why T dislikes him so.

Jez skipped quickly through the long passages of description and list of balls, drums and routs, shopping trips and morning calls.

May 11ᵗʰ

Her Grace of A called, to see me. She invites me to join her party to Vauxhall gardens tomorrow night. I can scarce believe my good fortune. Our cousin says it is a great honour to be noticed. Thomas will not go with me. He is attending a lecture at the Royal Academy, but sees no harm in it. Her Grace has promised to send me her spare domino and a mask to wear for the occasion. I can scarce contain myself at such a treat!

Jez read the next few pages, then went back over them more carefully. For all her excited anticipation, Sarah had written nothing about Vauxhall—did she not go, or was the experience less enjoyable than she had expected? Frowning, Jez read on.

May 18th.

Sunday. We accompanied Lady Marcham to morning service at St Martin's. Papa would be shocked at the congregation, so few attend to the sermon and I think most are there only to show off their finery and to gossip. My new tawny overdress and matching bonnet were as fine as any there, I believe.

May 23rd

Our cousin takes me to the ridotto tonight. I wish Thomas would go with me. If R is there, how shall I respond?

May 27th

I have remained in the house for several days together. Lady Marcham begins to grow suspicious. Perhaps I should tell her the truth, but I fear she would laugh at my scruples, for she says Thomas and I are quite rustic. I dare not tell

T. If he should challenge R, my poor husband would be no match for him. How I wish I could go home. We dine tonight with Mrs. Howard and go on to Lady Cochrane's rout. I cannot avoid it.

May 28ᵗʰ

I cannot tell a soul of my troubles, yet I must pour out my sorrow or I shall grow mad. Therefore, journal, you must be my confidante. I cannot avoid R while we are in Town, but despite his entreaties since Vauxhall I have refused to grant him a private audience. Last night at Lady Cochrane's he told me he has information of great import that we must discuss. He says it concerns my husband and the very future of my family. Thomas attends a meeting of the Royal Astronomical Society this evening, so I shall tell our cousin that I have no mind to go out. I have given him leave to call.

There was a break at this point, and Jez noted that in the next faded entry, the writing became much more ragged. It was difficult to read but she struggled on, only to turn the page and find there were no more entries in the journal. She quickly leafed through the remaining crackling pages but the blank paper seemed to jeer at her. Hastily she put the book aside and pulled out the bundles of letters, quickly scanning them, and going back to read some again more carefully.

She was so engrossed in her task that she did not notice the gradual lightening of the sky or the sound of a shuffling step in the passage.

"Jessica? My dear girl what are you doing?"

Emmy hobbled into the lounge, staring at her niece, who was sitting on the floor surrounded by sheets of yellowed paper. Jez looked up and Emmy was startled to see the tears coursing down her cheeks.

"My poor girl, what is it?"

"I know what she did, Aunt Emmy. I know now why she never saw her children again."

Chapter Eleven

Sarah heard the scrunch of carriage wheels on the road outside and ran to the window to peep through the shutters. Although she could not see his face, there was no mistaking the elegant figure in velvet and lace who descended from the carriage. She resumed her seat and picked up her embroidery. She would not let him see how nervous she was. When he was shown in she rose and made him a little curtsey but did not offer her hand.

"Lord Cordeaux!" She managed a fair assumption of surprise. "Lady Marcham is gone out, my lord, and m-my husband also."

"I know that, you minx, you told me it would be so."

Her cheeks flamed. If he could disregard the footman in the room then so could she. She said haughtily, "You said you had something to tell me, my lord."

He raised his brows.

"So cold and formal, madam?"

The quizzical look in his eyes made her knees weak. She resumed her seat.

"What else should I be." She glanced towards the lackey standing sphinx-like by the door. There was no impropriety; even the Earl of Cordeaux would not ravish her before a servant. Would he? "Tell me what you have to say, sir. I have no wish to prolong this meeting."

He took out his snuff box.

"I want you to reconsider my offer, Lady Methven."

"Impossible, my lord. You have my final answer."

"But is it?" He helped himself to a pinch of snuff, then slowly dusted his fingers upon his snowy handkerchief. His unhurried air wound her nerves to screaming pitch. "You might wish to think a little more about it, my lady, when I tell you I have in my possession some letters written by your husband to one Robert Murray. Your husband's cousin, I believe."

Sarah froze. The earl was smiling, but the steeliness in his gaze unnerved her. She addressed the footman.

"You may go. Wait in the hall. I shall call for you if I need you." She waited until the door had closed behind the servant before continuing. "Yes, Murray is Thomas' cousin, but we have not seen him for many years."

"He is a supporter of the Stuart, is he not?"

She began to fan herself vigorously.

"I really could not say."

"No? But your husband knows it. He was foolish enough to write to Murray before the forty-five, declaring his support for the Pretender."

She jumped up. "I do not believe you!"

"No?" He pulled a folded paper from his pocket and held it out to her. "Look at it, madam. Look at it carefully and tell me if that is not your husband's hand."

Sarah snatched the paper and peered at it, turning it so that the light from the candles played upon the page. Her fingers trembled.

"Where did you get this?"

The earl waved a hand.

"There are few things that money cannot buy. You will admit, the contents of that letter alone are enough to damn your husband. And I have several others, all of them showing that he was ready to declare himself for the Prince if he should march on London. If these letters were to fall into the—er—wrong hands, Sir Thomas would be imprisoned as a traitor and The Crown would seize his estate."

She sank down into her chair, a cold chill stealing around her heart.

"And the children..."

"Paupers, madam. Worse. Outcasts. Who would dare to befriend them?"

She stared up into his face.

"And you would do this. You would ruin us—me—because I refuse to be your mistress?"

"You have driven me to it, madam," he said harshly. "I must have you."

In a fury she jumped to her feet.

"Then take me," she hissed at him. She threw her arms wide. "Here I am. We are alone. Take me here, now, then for pity's sake leave me in peace!"

The violence of her outburst shocked her. The earl did not move.

"You do not understand, Sarah," he said quietly. "I do not want you for one quick coupling. I would have you live with me, night and day."

"For how long?"

"Until this madness passes." The anger left his face. He crossed the room and put his hands on her shoulders, pushing her back into her chair and dropping to his knees before her.

101

He said gently, "I have tried to forget you, Sarah, but I cannot. You haunt my dreams." He reached out and caught her hands, the letter falling away unnoticed. "There is a bond between us, Sarah. I feel it when you are near me, I see it in your eyes. You know it as well as I."

"No! I am married, my lord!"

"An arrangement, merely. A contract with a man almost twice your age, and one moreover who does not appreciate you. Tell me, Sarah, does he make your spirit sing, do you tremble when he holds your hands—does he even *hold* your hands as I am doing now?"

"Oh, stop," cried Sarah. "Thomas is a good man. He is no traitor: he does not deserve to be ruined."

"You can save him from that disgrace, Sarah. I will give you all the letters, for a price."

"And—and the price?"

"Come to me. Live with me as my mistress."

Sarah looked into his face. The temptation was very great. She could not deny the pull of attraction, the pleasure she experienced in his company. She put out one hand and gently touched his cheek. He turned his head slightly to kiss her wrist. He was rich and handsome, accustomed to getting his own way. She thought that perhaps she was the first one ever to deny him anything. She said softly, "Would you jeopardise your soul and mine, sir?"

He rose, his face once more a cold and indifferent mask. "I will do whatever is necessary to possess you."

"Then God forgive me for having roused such a monster."

"You have until midnight tomorrow," he said, striding to the door. "If I do not have your answer by then, the letters will pass out of my possession." He bowed. "Until tomorrow, Lady

Methven."

Leaving Lady Marcham's house was easier than Sarah had dared to imagine. Thomas had decided they should leave for Burford the next day, and he was dining out with his friends that night. Lady Marcham accepted Sarah's plea of a headache without demur—in fact, she said, Sarah's pale face and haunted eyes had been worrying her for some days. Wrapping herself in her travelling cloak, Sarah slipped unseen from a side door and made her way through the dark, wet streets, arriving at Cordeaux House just as the bells at the nearby church were striking eleven.

As she reached the heavy iron gates, her courage failed her and she clung for a moment to the glistening ironwork, her bare fingers curling around the intricately carved iron roses that were interwoven between the bars, but they were cold and unyielding to her touch. Taking a steadying breath, she crossed the drive and knocked upon the heavy oak door. A surprised footman admitted her to the marbled hallway where she waited for another servant to summon his master.

Lord Cordeaux descended the elegant curving staircase to find a diminutive cloaked figure in the centre of the hall. She had thrown back her hood, and her red-gold curls tumbled over her shoulders.

"My dear Lady Methven, why have my doltish servants left you here? They should have shown you to the morning room—"

"Sir, I would enter no further until I had spoken to you."

He took her hands and looked down at the pale face.

"Why, child, you are trembling."

She put up her chin, meeting his eyes with an unwavering look.

"Yesterday, sir, you offered me an—an exchange."

"I did, madam."

Her courage began to wane. She fixed her gaze upon the diamond nestled in the folds of snowy lace at his throat.

"Um—I would not have my husband ruined, my lord." Glancing up, she caught the flash of triumph in his eyes.

"It is not necessary that he should be, madam."

"And you will give me the letters?"

"As soon as I have your word that you will be mine, Sarah."

"You have it, sir. I am here."

"And you will not leave me?"

"No, my lord. You have my solemn word. I will remain with you until you release me from my vow."

He kissed her hand and held it tightly. "Oh Sarah, Sarah, I shall never let you go!" With an exultant laugh he swept her up into his arms and carried her upstairs.

Sarah lay passively in his arms as he bore her upwards, past the grand reception rooms and on to his bedchamber. She turned her head to hide her burning face against his chest as they passed liveried footmen at the stop of the stairs. She felt the rumble of his laugh against her cheek.

"Shy, little love?"

"Ashamed!" she replied, her voice muffled.

His arms tightened. How was it possible, she wondered, to be comforted by those strong arms around her and at the same time to feel so much guilt?

"Open the door!"

A footman jumped to obey the earl's command and Sarah peeped round to see that he had carried her into a sumptuous apartment, illuminated only by a blazing fire. Panic welled up as he strode towards a bed hung about with red and gold curtains and surmounted by a magnificent gilded tester. At the last moment he swung away and put her down gently in a huge winged chair beside the fire. Sarah did not move. She stared at the flames while the earl barked his orders and sent his servants hurrying away to do his bidding. When they were alone he sat down beside her on a low stool.

"Did you think I was going to throw you on the bed and ravish you?" He took her hands, gently circling his thumbs against the soft skin of each wrist. "I am not so inconsiderate a lover."

Sarah ran her tongue across her dry lips. Her experience of lovemaking was restricted to Thomas' infrequent and clumsy coupling. She was sure the earl would require something more of her. She fixed her anxious gaze upon him.

"I do not know—" Her face burned hot again. "What do you want me to do?"

He lifted her hand and pressed a kiss into the palm.

"For now I require nothing more than your company. Talk to me, Sarah. Entertain me."

Once she started talking, she found it easy enough to converse with the earl while soft-footed servants came in and set a variety of dishes and decanters on a small table. Their commonplace talk was no different from the idle discourse she had held with many a stranger at the dinner table, and it helped to relax her. The earl coaxed her to drink a glass of claret, and gradually the wine and the warmth of the fire had its effect. She untied the strings of her cloak and pushed it from her shoulders. She also stopped casting anxious looks over her shoulder at the shadowed bed. Lord Cordeaux dismissed the servants and held out his hand to her.

"Come sit at the table, my dear. We will sup together."

There were fresh fruits, potted meats and succulent chicken cooked in wine. The earl was very attentive, coaxing her to eat and Sarah found herself growing more at ease with him. He even surprised a laugh from her.

"That's much better," he said, refilling her glass. "This is your life now, Sarah I would not have you unhappy."

"What if I do not...please you?" she asked, not looking at him.

He came around the table and took her hand, pulling her to her feet.

"I think that is very unlikely."

He tried to pull her into his arms but she put her hands against his chest and held him off.

"And Thomas' letters?"

He pointed to a carved wooden box on the overmantel.

"They are all in there. Do you want to look at them?"

"No. I trust you, my lord."

His mouth twisted into a bitter smile.

"Do you? Even though I forced you here against your will?"

"It is better if we do not think of that, if you please."

With a shaky laugh he caught her to him and kissed her ruthlessly. It was everything she remembered, the heady scent of sandalwood on his skin, the liquefying touch of his lips on hers. She forgot everything—there was no past, no future, only Richard. Richard holding her, kissing her, undressing her. He joked that he was more adept than many a lady's maid as he unlaced her stays.

"Scarlet ribbons, too," he murmured as he pulled the stays away and dropped them to the floor. "Is that in my honour?"

Sarah blushed and he laughed at her. His hands rested on

her shoulders. Gently he pushed aside the chemise and lowered his mouth to her neck, his lips trailing kisses along her collar bone. She shuddered delightfully. Her body was coming alive beneath his hands, responding to his touch, and when at last he lifted her into his arms and carried her to the bed she was not afraid of the dark, cavernous shadows. She lay in the darkness, excitement growing as she watched Richard shed his clothes. She caught her breath at the sight of his lean body. It gleamed in the firelight and she found herself reaching out for him, pulling him onto the bed, onto her.

Sarah had never experienced such pleasure in a man's touch. At last she knew what it was to be loved, worshipped. Richard's hands explored her gently and she wrapped herself around him, exulting in the feel of his hard body pressing against hers, skin on skin. When, finally, he entered her, she cried out, arching her body, clinging tightly to him as they fell together through time and space.

As the first grey fingers of dawn crept into the room, Sarah crouched before the fire, feeding the glowing embers with strips of crackling parchment. They wrinkled and blackened, then flared with a brief, bright flame. The letters were destroyed. Her body ached from a night of frantic lovemaking. Richard had taken her, time and again, and she had revelled in it, succumbing to the overwhelming passion and marvelling at her own power. But now, in the cold chill of early morning she was wracked with guilt.

Thomas and the children were safe. Yet at what price to her soul?

Chapter Twelve

Jez handed the ancient book to Emmy.

"It's all here in her journal, Auntie!" She wiped a hand across her tear-stained face. "Sarah met some rich lord in London, he fell in love with her and blackmailed her into leaving her husband—"

"Hush, love, you said you wanted me to read if for myself."

Jez sat back and sipped at her tea, trying to curb her impatience. Emmy had refused to do anything more until she had made them both a hot drink. Jez wondered why she had not asked for coffee—she always had coffee in the mornings at home. At least she had done so until Piers had made her a cup of Earl Grey—she thrust the thought of Piers from her mind.

"So you think she ran off with this *R* person?" asked Emmy.

"Yes. That letter I read to you yesterday"—Jez sorted through the letters—"this one, where she asked Thomas to allow her to see her children—'I know I have sinned most grievously.' She is obviously not living with them, she even says...where is it...'I did not willingly abandon you.'" She handed the letter to her aunt then sat back, wrapping her hands around her cup. "I felt such an affinity with Sarah, Aunt Emmy! And—and I feel that I already *know* her story! It's like reading a book after seeing the film, it's so familiar..."

Emmy shook her head. "Nonsense, child. You're just putting two and two together. After all, it's pretty plain from the letters—"

"No, no, I'm not guessing, auntie. Somehow I *know* this story."

"I suppose it is possible that your mother has heard this tale and discussed it in your hearing, when you were very little. *I've* never heard it mentioned in the family."

Jessica shivered. "When I read her letters, her anguish at not being allowed to see her children—it—it's barbaric!"

"You must remember this was two hundred and sixty years ago, Jez. Life was much harsher then. Religion was taken very seriously, and adultery was a mortal sin."

Jez lifted another letter.

"But read this one, Emmy! Because her family disowned her, she was forced to accept charity from the man who had ruined her."

> *Lilac Cottage*
>
> *July 1748*
>
> *Sir,*
>
> *You are aware that only the direst necessity would make me write to you. While I am grateful for your bounty in allowing me the use of this house, I had hoped to throw myself upon the mercy of my family for my future provision. Alas, I was mistaken in the belief that there was any Christian forgiveness to be received there. It would appear that I have sinned too deeply to be returned to the bosom of my family, or even to live in its shadow. My father prays daily for my soul*

but cannot allow such a sinful influence to cross his threshold. My husband has written to inform me that he has ordered all memory of me to be erased from his household. He begs I will importune him no further.

I am therefore thrown back upon your mercy, my lord. My fate, if you will not aid me, is too hideous to contemplate. I have no right to expect you to continue to look kindly upon one who refuses to grant you any form of intercourse, but you are my last hope and I must accept, albeit reluctantly, the small provision that you once offered me, that I may live out my days with some small measure of independence.

My prayers, as always, are for your happiness and redemption. Your soul, I believe, is not irrevocably lost to God, for I know you to be a good man at heart. I remain, sir, your humble and grateful servant

S M

Emmy stared at Jez. "You've seen the address at the top of this letter?"

Jez nodded. "Lilac Cottage. Do—do you think it's the same one?"

"Well, it's been in the family for generations, and we believe Sarah is a relative of ours—it seems very likely."

"What I don't understand," said Jez, frowning, "is how this letter came to be in the box with all the others. After all, it's to this unknown lord."

Emmy handed her the letter. "It is not so well written, and it is folded just once, in half. It's a copy, Jez. Sarah may have written it out in rough first. Remeber, this was a very difficult letter for her to write."

"But look, Emmy, it says, 'I am grateful for your bounty in allowing me the use of this house'—so Lilac Cottage belonged to this lord, whoever he was. Wow, that's so eerie. To think of the poor woman in my house. I wonder if we can find out more about her, and find out who this mysterious *R* can be."

§

"Harry! I'm back—just wait 'til you hear—" Jez broke off, laughing. "Oh, my God! You look like an alien. Just what have you been doing?"

Harry had emerged from the dining room. A thick film of pale grey dust covered him from head to foot, except for two white rings around his eyes where he had removed his goggles. "Hacking off the plaster, like you wanted. Come and see."

She dropped her bags and followed him into the dining room.

"I've virtually finished, only a bit more in that corner to take off."

Jez was not listening. She was staring at the centre of the wall where Harry's hard work had exposed two large upright blocks of stone.

"Hey, look at this—it could be the supports of an old fireplace. And look, it's rough stone around it, but the centre has been bricked up." She turned to Harry, her eyes shining. "Do you think we could open it up?"

He shrugged. "Don't see much point, it's all been filled in."

"But what a great feature. We could dig out all that brick, it won't take long. I'll go and get changed and give you a hand."

He caught her arm to detain her. "Oh no, I've had enough for one day. I'll get showered and we'll have a drink."

By the time they sat down in the lounge, relaxing with a glass of wine, the idea of opening up the fireplace was growing on Harry.

"I suppose it would add value to the place. I wonder how old it is?"

"Well, Emmy and I think we found evidence this weekend that someone was living here in the mid-eighteenth century. This could be the very fireplace she used to sit by."

"She?"

"Sarah Methven. She lived here after she left her husband. She ran away to become the mistress of some lord."

"Oho, skeletons in the family cupboard, eh, Jez?"

She shifted uncomfortably.

"Don't joke about it, Harry, it ruined the poor woman. I just wonder what it would be like, to see the fireplace as it used to be in her day."

"Well don't get too carried away. There's a lot of labouring to do yet to get all those bricks out."

With the excitement of finding the letters and uncovering the fireplace, Jez found she had plenty to keep her occupied the following week, and she could almost convince herself that the night with Piers had never happened—until Harry found the dress. He was searching through the wardrobes for a missing shirt when he gave a long whistle.

"Hey, what's this?"

"Hmm? Oh that. It's mine."

"Well I guessed that much! But Jez, this must have cost a bomb, and you know we agreed to keep our spending down—"

"No, no, you don't understand! It came out of CME's exhibition budget. Everyone is expected to look like a million dollars." She laughed. "They even called it a uniform, but since it's no good to anyone else, I get to keep it."

She smothered her prickling conscience—it wasn't too far from the truth.

"Huh, I always knew I should have gone into marketing instead of engineering." He glanced at the clock beside the bed. "Christ, is that the time? I'm going to be late—and I really wanted to be in early today. There's some new projects in the pipeline and I want to be in on them."

With a brief kiss he was gone, the dress forgotten, except that Jez was uncomfortably aware she was not telling the whole truth.

Jez spotted the Porsche as she drove into the car park. There had been no announcement of a new sales director being appointed, so when Piers walked into the office she was prepared. A small, distant smile was all she gave him, then it was head down and on with her work. Perfect.

But she was painfully aware of him as he discussed a report with Lavinia, and when he left the room she had to acknowledge her disappointment that he had not even tried to speak to her. The phone on her desk buzzed.

"Jez?" It was Piers.

"Yes?"

"Just wanted to say hi. How are you?"

"Fine, thank you."

"Things going well with Harry?"

"Yes, of course."

"Then I suppose dinner is out of the question?"

She smiled at his persistence. "I'm afraid so."

"Then just a drink somewhere after work?"

"Sorry. I can't."

"Can't or won't?"

"Both. I am in fact very busy. Please don't pressure me."

"Sorry. I'm not used to refusals."

"Then stop asking." She looked up to find Lavinia watching her. She sat up and tried to sound more businesslike. "Look, I'm sorry I can't help you, sir. I can only suggest that you try elsewhere."

She put the phone down.

"Who was that?"

"One of these survey companies. Wanted me to answer tons of questions. They really are getting too pushy."

Chapter Thirteen

Jez stood in the little dining room and gazed at the rough stone and brickwork. The plaster had been removed now to reveal an ancient oak crossbeam to the fireplace. Her thoughts ran back over the letters she had read at her aunt's house. Poor Sarah, she must have been so unhappy, disowned by her family, barred from her kids—what a high price to pay for her infidelity. Jez could almost picture her, sitting in this very room, weeping for her lost virtue while her lover hammered on the door, begging to see her—

"Oh!"

A sudden loud banging on the front door made her start violently, and she felt the hairs at the back of her neck rise. She tried to laugh at herself for being so fanciful but her heart was still hammering painfully against her ribs as she answered the impatient summons.

"Harry! What on earth—!"

"Hell, Jez, I thought you'd gone out." Harry brushed past her. "I forgot my key—and the bloody bell doesn't work. God, it's cold out there! Is food ready?"

She bit back an acid retort. "Have a look in the kitchen, there's some cold meat and stuff. I didn't know what time you'd be home, so I grabbed a sandwich when I got in. I'm due at the restaurant in ten minutes."

uot;Sorry, I didn't think to ring you—last minute meeting." He grinned. "They've asked me to go to Germany."

"Germany!"

"Yes, I'm on the team to set up the new project at their offices just outside Cologne."

"Oh Harry, that's great news." Her irritation evaporated in the face of his excitement. "When do you go?"

"Monday."

"What!"

"I know it's a rush, but they want everything up and running before the end of the year."

"So—how long will you be away?"

"Three weeks, initially."

"But Harry, that takes us right up to Christmas!"

He kissed her and patted her cheek. "I know love, but it's the chance I've been waiting for. I can't refuse to go."

"I know that, but—"

"And besides, you know what it's like at the restaurant at Christmas, all those extra shifts, and now that you're working at CME as well you'll be too busy to miss me."

"Oh, Harry, you know that's not true! Look, I've got to go or I'll be late. We'll talk about this when I get back."

"Fine." He was already turning away. "Did you say there was food in the kitchen?"

"Jez, table four is ready to order now."

"What? Oh, sorry! I'm on my way."

"Are you all right love?" Malcolm, the owner of the Spinning Wheel Restaurant glanced keenly at Jessica when she returned and handed him the order.

116

"What? Oh, yes. Sorry, I'm just a bit pre-occupied tonight. Harry came home and told me he's off to Germany on Monday. For three weeks."

"That's a bit sudden. Will you miss him?"

"Of course, but what's really annoying is that we've just started some work on the cottage. First time Harry's ever got involved in anything like that, and now he's going away and there's no chance it will be finished by Christmas. It means the whole room is out of action." She gave him a wry smile. "Still, I suppose with Harry away I won't need much room anyway."

"Can't you go with him?"

"Pardon?"

"Take some time off and go with him. If his company's paying for the accommodation you'd only have to find your fare and food money."

"I hadn't thought of that. It's an idea, if not this time then when he goes back in the spring—he says it's going to be a long project."

Malcolm inspected the glass he was polishing before putting it away behind the little bar in the corner.

"You should consider it," he said. "You can pick up flights to Europe very cheaply now." He glanced over her shoulder. "Another customer. Off you go."

She made her way between the small candlelit tables but her welcoming smile vanished as she recognised the new diner. She struggled to maintain her composure, readjusted her smile but could not resist a muttered question through her clenched teeth. "What are you doing here?"

Piers Cordeaux smiled at her, his dark eyes glinting. "I thought I'd grab a meal before heading back to London."

"But this isn't on your route."

"You don't know that."

"Did you know I worked here?"

"Yes. You told me, remember?"

She shut her lips tightly, resisting the provocation. *He's just another customer*, she told herself. *Be professional.* "Are you dining alone, sir?"

"Unless you're free to join me."

Ignoring that, she handed him the menu. "I'll leave you to choose your meal."

She turned away, hoping her face did not give away the confusion of thoughts and emotions she was feeling. Fortunately the restaurant was busy so she had no time to worry about Piers, but as she served her customers she wondered why he had come. She couldn't deny his attraction, nor the illicit feeling of pleasure at the thought that he had come to see her, but it was cruel of him to do it, when she was trying so hard to forget him. Reluctantly she returned to take his order.

"Would you like to see the wine list?"

He flashed a glance at her, a mocking gleam in his blue eyes that dissolved her insides and turned her knees to jelly.

"I seem to remember you know a bit about wines," he murmured. "What would you suggest?"

"Water, if you're driving," she muttered savagely.

He grinned. "Quite right. I'll have a mineral water."

She stalked to the back of the restaurant. Malcolm grinned at her. "Oho, who's rattled your cage?"

Damn Malcolm, he could be far too observant. "Oh, just someone I know from CME. Thinks a lot of himself."

"The guy in the corner? He looks vaguely familiar."

"Yeah, like those super smoothies on the chocolate ads. Too good to be true." She handed over Piers' order. "Nevertheless, he's quite influential at CME, so let's make sure his salmon is perfect—it could be good for your business."

Later, from the back of the restaurant she watched as Malcolm made his rounds, chatting to his customers, joking with the regulars and checking that everyone was happy. He paused by Piers' table and seemed to stay there much longer than normal.

She waited uneasily until Malcolm returned. "Everything okay?"

"Yes, no problem. Your friend has no complaints, he even sends his compliments to the chef!" He grinned, and Jez knew he was thinking of Jason, his partner, cooking away in the tiny kitchen below stairs. "Nice guy."

He was watching her closely, and she was careful not to react.

"Would you like a sweet, sir?" she avoided Piers' eyes as she cleared his table.

"Just coffee, thank you. Then I'd better be going. I enjoyed the meal. Is it always this good?"

"Yes. Malcolm and his partner prepare it all themselves."

"Excellent. They'd make a fortune in London."

"They moved here to get away from the big city. Not everyone lives to make money."

"Ouch. Was that aimed at me?"

She flushed.

"No. Sorry." She risked looking at him and knew immediately it was a mistake. His eyes held her glance for a long moment, and she felt he was reading her deepest thoughts.

At last she forced herself to look away and gathered up the dishes, her trembling hands making them rattle alarmingly. "I'll get your coffee and the bill."

The entrance of a large party of diners caused a welcome diversion, and Jez persuaded Malcolm to serve Piers while she dealt with the newcomers. By the time she had settled the party at two tables, taken their coats and organised their first drinks, Piers had left. Glancing at the empty table in the corner, she thought of him making the long drive back to London alone and found herself regretting that she had not at least wished him a safe journey.

By the end of the evening Jez was desperately tired. She cleared up mechanically and set the tables ready for the following day, then went back to collect her coat.

Malcolm had just finished cashing up. "Here. Your wages for the night—and tips."

She stared at the notes in her hand. "This can't be right!"

"Oh it is, love. Your friend left a fifty pound tip." Malcolm smiled. "Don't be silly about it, girl, no need to look so offended. It's honestly earned—and it will pay for your air fare to Germany."

Chapter Fourteen

Unbricking the fireplace was proving to be more difficult than Jez had expected. The bricks were tightly packed into the frame of the old fireplace with very little mortar between them, so removing the first brick was tough work. After that, she reasoned, it would get easier, with more room to loosen the bricks. She chipped away steadily at the mortar, prising it out until at last the first brick could be tapped loose and removed.

Her flagging enthusiasm was renewed as she quickly tapped out two more bricks. The gap revealed a sooty black hole filled with rubble. Jez stood for a moment, looking at her handiwork. She was aware of the silence in the house and felt a faint nervousness, reminiscent of those horror movies where something unspeakable crawls out of the blackness, disturbed by unwitting humans...

She screamed as something touched her shoulder.

"Hey, girl, what's wrong?"

"Oh, Harry!" She threw her arms around him, narrowly missing his ear with the lump hammer she was still holding, "Oh, you made me jump."

"Obviously. Why didn't you wake me if you wanted to make a start on this?"

"I didn't like to—you got home so late last night, I thought I'd let you sleep. Did the hammering disturb you? Sorry."

"No, it's time I was up, anyway. I've got some shopping to do for the trip on Monday. How about coming with me?"

Her heart leapt. "To Germany, you mean?"

"No, stupid! Shopping."

"Oh. Oh—yes. Fine. Just let me get changed. Harry—I *could* go with you, you know. It wouldn't cost a lot, just the air fare and meals..."

He kissed her.

"I'd love to have you along, Jez, you know that, but we're going to be really busy setting up this project. Besides, even I don't know where we're staying yet. Let's wait 'til I go back in the spring and maybe we can arrange for you to come over for a few days then. How does that sound to you?"

"Okay." Jez tried to stifle her disappointment. After all, it was a sensible arrangement. Only she didn't want to be sensible.

"Poor love. It's only for a few weeks, and I'll be back for Christmas. That's not so bad, is it?"

She summoned up a smile. "No, of course not. Come on, then. I'll get changed and we can go buy you a toothbrush."

§

"Hello, Jessica? It's Aunt Emmy."

"Emmy! How lovely to hear from you! How are you? How's that foot?"

"Oh it's fine now. The doctor took off the strapping this week but he says I mustn't overdo it. No marathons or anything. How are you? Have you finished the fireplace?"

Jez stifled a sigh. "No way. Harry's gone off to Germany for his company and won't be back until Christmas. I've taken out a few more bricks but it's full of rubble behind there, so it's very slow, especially since I'm working such a lot now."

She didn't mention that she only liked to work in the room during daylight. She knew it was fanciful, but she really did not like being in the dining room alone during the evening, uncovering that dark hole.

"I thought I'd give you a ring to let you know how I'm getting on with my researches."

"About Sarah and the letters you mean? I have to confess, Auntie, that I've done nothing at all this end. I haven't even looked at the church records."

"That's understandable. You young people today are so busy with your work and everything. But anyway, I think we can be sure she is a relative. I checked back in the church records in Burford, and Sarah Appleton did marry a Thomas Methven in 1742. Interestingly, it says his father was a baronet—Sir Angus Methven from Aberdeen."

"So there *is* a Scottish connection—you remember, she said there were letters from Thomas in support of the Jacobite rebellion!"

"Yes. And there are records of two christenings—Jennifer Sarah Methven in 1743 and Thomas Henry in 1744."

"The children she was forced to abandon. Is there anything else, Emmy?"

"Only entries in the parish registers, nothing to add to the story and no other mention of Sarah. But going back to the marriage records, he was forty when he married Sarah. She was only eighteen."

"So?"

"Don't you think that's rather a large age gap?"

"Not if they were in love."

"But Jez, you must remember that in those days very few people even *lived* until they were forty. He would have been considered very old by the standards of the day."

"Well, perhaps she preferred older men. Or are you saying that she was not happy in her marriage?"

"Well, that's possible. At any rate she may have been more attracted to her rich lover than we first thought."

Jez frowned. "I don't know, Emmy. She was strongly religious, and I think she took her marriage very seriously. She knew there was no happiness to be found if she broke her vows."

"That sounds more like your own opinion." Her aunt's voice was gentle, but Jez flushed.

"It *is* my opinion. You know how I feel about infidelity in a relationship."

"Is that why you won't go to stay with your mother and her new husband?"

"I'm sure Bruno is very nice, Aunt Emmy, but I know he was on the scene even before Dad died—"

"But darling, people change. They can fall out of love, you know, as well as into it."

"A promise is a promise, Emmy. You can't just make a commitment then walk away from it."

"Even if it is making everyone unhappy? Oh Jessica, you are as stubborn and idealistic as your father."

"There's nothing wrong with that."

"Nothing at all, love, but we are human, after all, and can't all live up to your high ideals. Oh heavens, let's not fight. Tell me instead when you are coming to see me again."

"After Christmas, Emmy, I promise. And I'll do my best to

find some information on Sarah and Lilac Cottage."

Chapter Fifteen

Spurred into action by her conversation with her aunt, Jez decided to visit the local records office the very next week. It took several telephone calls to ascertain that the records she needed were in Filchester, and she made an appointment to see the archivist the following week. A quick phone call to Kate and she arranged to meet her friend for lunch the same day.

"And I'm really glad we *could* meet," said Jez as she finished her salad. Her eyes strayed to the remains of the creamy tagliatelle in Kate's dish. She envied her friend's ability to eat mountains of food and still stay rake-thin. "Apart from this, the morning's a complete disappointment."

"Didn't you find anything on the cottage?"

"Very little. It was really frustrating. Various disasters over the centuries mean that the records are incomplete. There's some evidence that the area in and around Luxbury belonged to the church in the Middle Ages, but there is no record of Lilac Cottage until the nineteenth century. There's an entry showing that rent was being paid to a Mistress Philippa Methven Grant in 1810."

"Well, that's a help isn't it? She has the Methven name."

"It's intriguing, but I don't know who she is. I suppose I could ring Aunt Emmy and ask her to look back through her papers..."

Kate scooped up the last of the tagliatelle.

"Know what I'd do? Call in at the parish church. There could be something in their records about her and any other members of the family who lived there."

"Of course! Why didn't I think of that? Kate, you're a genius. I'll pop in there this afternoon."

"Right." Kate rose. "Must dash, I've an appointment in ten minutes. Here." She threw a couple of notes onto the table. "Pay for the meal out of that. My treat for an impoverished student. 'Bye!"

She was gone before Jez could remonstrate, so Jez dutifully paid the waiter and made her way back to Luxbury.

Luxbury Parish Church stood alongside the main road through the old village with a set of iron railings separating it from the pavement. Inside the small porch was a notice indicating that a church had stood on the site since Saxon times, but the main structure had been rebuilt after a major fire in 1868. She spent a long time poring over the Parish Register before she found an entry that interested her. There was no mention of Philippa Methven Grant, but looking back at the earlier records, Jez found an entry for Sarah Methven, who died in 1780, aged fifty-seven years.

She was alone in the Church vestry, staring at the entry, and a sudden chill made her shudder. The noise of the cars on the main road intruded into the quiet stillness of the old building, like some rhythmic chant, *Sarah, Sarah...*

Shivering, Jez buttoned her coat and made her way towards the main door of the church, where she was met by the vicar coming in with armfuls of holly. He smiled as he sidestepped out of her way.

"Christmas decorations," he said, by way of an explanation.

127

"Find everything you need?"

"Yes, thanks. Tell me, is there a catalogue of the gravestones?"

The old man shook his head, his faded blue eyes smiling at her through the thick lenses of his glasses.

"I'm sorry. Our local history group has talked about it, but it is very much in the early stages." He shrugged, dropping some of the greenery on the floor. "I'm afraid all you can do is look around the graveyard."

"And if I was looking for an old gravestone—say eighteenth century?"

The vicar was bending down, collecting up the scattered flora, and his face was pink with the exertion when he straightened up.

"What's that? Oh—oh well, now let me see... Probably in the far corner, just past the wooden bench. The oldest graves are in that area, but be careful, the path is a little overgrown and uneven there."

She stepped out into the cold and pulled her scarf a little closer. The sounds of the traffic were muted here, for the great bulk of the church separated the graveyard from the main road. The short wintry day was ending and a chill breeze rustled the trees. Rooks cawed noisily from their empty branches.

Jez walked amongst the gravestones, scanning them rapidly for Sarah's name. It was not easy, for they were very worn, some almost illegible. She found it at last on a grey slab in a very damp and shady corner. It was the only headstone in that area. The granite-grey stone was covered in ivy, which Jez pulled aside. She traced her fingers over the worn lettering, whispering the words as she deciphered them.

"Here lieth Sarah Appleton Methven, beloved mother of Thomas and Jennifer...died in the year of our lord 1780, aged

57 years... Judge not..."

Jez went back to the little bench and sat down, staring at the headstone and thinking hard. "Beloved mother"—did that mean she had been reunited with her children before her death? Or had they merely been informed that she was dead and had done their duty by her? How could she find out?

"Yer, what're you doin'? That ivy's protection for that there 'eadstone!"

She swung around to see who was shouting. An old man was approaching, shuffling towards her. He wore a pair of faded moleskin trousers tucked into his thick woollen socks, a pair of very muddy brown boots and an old tweed jacket tied at the waist with string. As he drew closer, she became aware of a shiny red nose and a pair of bloodshot eyes set beneath bushy grey brows—all that was visible between the peak of his flat cap and the muffler that covered his chin.

"I'm sorry, I meant no harm—"

"Harm? No, that's what they all say, coming in 'ere with their cameras and notebooks, pulling aside the plants that's protected these 'ere stones since time long gone by. Records, pshaw! We don't need no records. It's all 'ere, in the stones."

"No, no, I'm not recording anything. I was looking for Sarah Methven."

"Lady Sarah?" He stepped up to peer short-sightedly at her. "Oh, so you'm back then!"

She laughed. "No, I've never been here before."

The old man stared at her.

"You ain't wantin' to wreck the grave?"

"No of course not. I think she might be a relative of mine. Who are you? Do you look after the graves?"

"In a manner of speakin' you might say that." The old man

came to sit beside her and Jez shifted along the bench, leaving a clear gap between them. Even so there was a strong smell of tobacco emanating from his person.

"Then why don't you keep the weeds cut in this corner? It's rather a mess, isn't it?"

He tapped his nose with one grimy finger. "Protection."

"Protection?"

"Protection from 'er."

It was becoming apparent to Jez that her companion was not quite sane. She edged away to the end of the bench.

"She might come back, see, at any time and I's got to be ready. I mustn't let her harm Lady Sarah. That's my job."

"And who gave you this job?"

He sniffed loudly.

"Me old man. Passed down, y'see, from father to son. It was 'is father's job before and 'is granfers." He took out a pipe and battered tobacco pouch and cast a bleary eye at her. "Have you time for a story, miss?"

Fascinated, Jez nodded.

"Long time ago it was, see, 'underds of yers. Lady Sarah lived in the village then and my old relative knew 'er. They say that everyone knew 'er. Lovely lady, kind and gentle, visiting the sick and comin' to church every Sunday—never missed, they say. Then when she died there was some argument about where she was to be buried. Her son wanted to take her back to the family vault, but the lady's own wishes was to be buried 'ere, where she lived so long. Any road, my relative, he was gravedigger then, see? Dicked in the nob, they said he was, but he was never so daft that 'e couldn't find hisself a good woman to be 'is wife and provide for his family—and the proof is that we is still here, after all these years." He lit his pipe and drew on it steadily, silently contemplating his impressive lineage.

"So—so your *relative* buried Sarah?"

"Aye, that's it. Well, 'e dug the 'ole, anyway. Parson did the burying, o' course. Whole village turned out, so they said, but then, just as the earth is being filled in and the mourners is about to go, a coach rolls up—great gilded thing with a crest on the side, and a madwoman gets out and runs to the grave where she starts cursing poor Sarah's name and swearing she'll have no rest. Well, Parson and Sarah's son 'as to restrain the poor woman, for she looks set to pull Sarah from her very coffin, crying all the time that our poor departed lady had stolen her husband, that she should not be buried with decent folk being as how she was a—"

He coughed. "My relative did pass on the words she used, miss, but I'll not use 'em in front of a young lady. Anyhow, a servant comes and carries the poor distraught lady away, she screaming all the while that she'll be avenged on Sarah. Well, you can imagine that Parson and Sarah's family was real cut-up about all this, the ladies was crying and Parson shakin' his head. The upshot is that poor Sarah's son comes up to my relative and slips him a purse. Asks him very gentlemanlike if he would be kind enough to watch over his mama's grave, since he would not be able to do so hisself. Just in case the lady came back, see? Now my relative, being a God-fearing Christian who knows his duty, would willingly have looked after the poor soul's last resting place and not asked a penny for doing so, but the gentleman insisted. 'Keep the purse, my good man,' he says, very civil-like, 'and put it to some good use.' So when my relative goes 'ome and looks in the purse he finds it full of gold pieces! Well, 'is wife—who is by way of blood and nature also my relative, of course—his wife she was in a bad way at that time, on her third confinement, so he uses the gold to pay the doctor to attend 'er, rather than the gin-sodden old midwife, and praise be if she wasn't delivered of a bouncing baby boy that my distant relative promptly christens Thomas, in honour of poor Sarah's son!"

The old man drew on his pipe again, then continued proudly, "And 'is father give the task of watching over Sarah's grave to that Thomas, a solemn duty that 'e carried out faithfully all his days and passed on to 'is own son Thomas, and so on down the line of my relatives until it comes to me, the present Thomas." He ended, beaming at Jessica over his muffler.

She felt that some response was required. "That—that's a wonderful story, Thomas. And have you ever had to protect the grave?"

"No, never." He shook his head sadly. "They say the old madwoman died soon after, bless her poor soul. We've continued our vigil, man and boy, like we promised, but no-one comes to this corner, save yourself, and the dook, of course."

"The—the duke?"

"Well, some sort of lord, he is. He comes every so often, to sit over the grave for a few hours. Always wears his blue velvet coat he does, and 'is sword. Was me great-granfer which named him dook, course we don't know who he is really—"

"Hang on! Your *great-grandfather* saw him?"

"Yes, he did that, miss. Many a time."

The hair on the back of Jessica's neck prickled.

"But—your great-grandfather must have been dead for..."

"Nigh on seventy year now. He passed on when I was a babe."

Jez dug her hands into the pockets of her coat to stop them shaking. "Then this, this duke that you see—"

"Oh he's a spirit, miss. What you might call a ghost. We've

seen 'im off and on for over a hunderd yers." The old man chuckled. "Surely, miss, you don't think I'm mad enough to believe a man can live for all that time? That would be crazy! No, he's a ghost, right enough, it'd be plain daft to think anything else."

"Yes," she agreed faintly. "Yes, I suppose it would."

"Well now, Thomas, what are you doing here, keeping this young lady sitting about in the cold?"

Jez jumped up from the bench at the sudden voice, relaxing only when she saw it was the vicar bearing down upon them through the gloom. He was beaming at them, but clearly intent upon leading her away. She went with him willingly, after muttering goodbye to the old man, who remained sitting on the bench to finish his pipe.

"Poor old Tom," said the vicar comfortably. "Has he been telling you his tales?"

"Yes, he was telling me about his relatives."

"Take no notice. He's as mad as a hatter. Runs in the family, of course, but he's harmless enough. He likes to potter around, so we pay him to cut the grass and do a spot of weeding around the graves, and he does a reasonable job, generally, although nothing will make him tidy up that far corner. Strange that. Did you find the stone you were looking for, by the way?"

"Yes. Yes I did, thank you. I—um—Thomas said there was a—a ghost in the churchyard."

"Did he? Well, maybe he's right. I've never seen it, but if Tom's happy to believe it, we'll let him carry on, shall we?"

Silently, she nodded, hunching her shoulders against the cold wind as they left the churchyard. The wind sighed in the trees behind them.

Ah, Sarah.

Chapter Sixteen

There was a cold draught blowing in from the hole in the dining room. Jez had removed as much of the brick and stone as she could, but the bottom layers of mortar and rubble were proving stubborn and she made little progress. Knowing Harry would be home in a few days, she shut the door on the room, filled the gap beneath the door with rags and left it.

A full week had passed and she had told no-one about her trip to Luxbury church. She kept going over the events of that afternoon in her head, trying to make sense of them. Everything the old man had told her had sounded so reasonable at the time, sitting beside him in the churchyard. But the longer she thought it over, the more convinced she was that it had been merely the ramblings of a confused old man. Perhaps it had been his idea of a joke. After all, no-one really believed in ghosts, did they?

It was the Saturday before Christmas and Harry was due home that evening. Ignoring the mess in the back room, Jez cleaned the rest of the house and bought a small Christmas tree, which she decorated with simple white bows and silver baubles while she listened to the nonstop Christmas carols on the radio.

The ringing of the doorbell interrupted her idyll and she

opened the door, still clutching a bauble and with several lengths of white ribbon around her neck. The caller, a young man, blinked.

"Er, Miss Skelton?"

"Yes."

"Miss Jessica Skelton?" He was staring at her and she realised she was still holding up the silver ball.

She grinned. "Christmas."

He gave a tight smile. "I'm just delivering your new car, Miss Skelton. Sign here please."

"My what?"

"Your new car, miss." He stepped back and she looked towards the road, where a canary yellow Porsche Boxster was parked at the curb, attracting a small crowd, mainly the boys who usually hung around the local take-away.

"But I haven't ordered a new car."

The man smiled, as though dealing with an imbecile. "Well, someone has decided to make your Christmas. Can you just sign here, miss, and I can hand over the keys."

"Who bought it?"

"I'm sorry, I don't have that information." He held out the clipboard and pen hopefully.

Jez had an insane desire to laugh. Piers was trying to bribe her! Did he think she would fall for such an outrageous gesture? She wouldn't take it. Couldn't take it.

Why not? asked a little demon in her head. *He can afford it.* She squashed the thought even as it formed. Besides, how could she explain it to Harry?

Staring at the car, Jez swallowed hard. "No, I'm sorry. I don't want it."

"Pardon?"

"Take it away. I don't want the car."

"But—but it's all paid for—you can't turn it down!"

"Oh yes I can."

He looked at her, then at the car, and back again at her, staring as though she were some kind of freak. He held out the pen again, his tone becoming a little desperate.

"But, miss—do you realise what *I* would do if someone gave me a Porsche?"

She smiled, took the pen and tucked it into his jacket pocket.

"For all I care, you can keep this one. I. Don't. Want. It. Goodbye."

"B-but it—it's beautiful. It's a *Porsche!*"

"No, thank you."

"But—"

His last words were lost as she shut the door and walked back into the lounge to finish decorating the tree. Through the window she saw him walking back to the car, shaking his head, and a few moments later he had gone.

Jez couldn't pretend that she was unmoved. There was only one person she knew with enough money to make such a gesture, but if he thought he could buy her with his expensive presents, he was very much mistaken. She fixed the star to the top of the tree and stood back to view the effect. She hoped he would ring her before Harry came home.

It was an hour later when the call came. "Jez?"

"Happy Christmas, Piers."

"Why did you reject my present?"

"You know very well I couldn't accept such a thing. How

would I explain it to Harry?"

"By telling him it's all over between you."

"But it's not. I don't think you understand, Piers. Harry and I have a commitment. I know you aren't very familiar with that concept, but it means you don't cheat on your partner."

"I don't want you to cheat on him. Just leave him."

"Goodbye Piers."

"Jez—"

She put the phone down, smiling.

"One up to me, I think."

Jez was still working on her report, papers spread out over the coffee table around the laptop, when she heard Harry come in.

"Hi, gorgeous!"

She jumped up to kiss him.

"Harry! Where have you been? You said the plane was landing at four."

"Yes, well, it did, love but I had to drop Charlie off on the way." He looked at her. "You're not mad, are you Jez? I said I might be late."

She shrugged. "I know, but I didn't think it would take you five hours to get here. I'll make some coffee. How was Cologne?"

"Freezing." He followed her into the kitchen. "Their winters are a lot colder than ours, you know." He lifted the lid from a pan. "What's this?"

"Bolognese. Don't worry. I had mine earlier. Just thought you might want some supper when you got home."

"That was thoughtful of you, but we ate at the airport. I needed something to wake me up. Hell, I'm tired."

"You're looking very well, though. Cologne must agree with you." He looked stockier than she remembered, but she thought it prudent not to ask him if he'd put on weight. "So when do you have to go back?"

"January tenth. It's great over there, Jez. You should see the office block—looks like something from an American movie, all polished chrome and glass. This job's going to take some time, so we're getting an apartment in Cologne next year."

"Great, that means I'll be able to come and stay with you." She handed him a mug.

"Yeah, once we've got it all settled." He led the way back into the lounge. "So what have you been doing with yourself?"

"Oh the usual, waitressing at the Spinning Wheel, working on my thesis and recommendations for my MSc. I want to get that finished by Christmas." Harry was flicking through the TV channels. She considered telling him about Piers and his gift of the Porsche, but decided against it. "I went to Luxbury churchyard and talked to a man about a ghost."

"Great, great."

With a sigh, she began to tidy her papers. She tried not to feel disappointed but there was a vague sense of anticlimax about the evening. She had not expected him to come home and jump on her, ripping her clothes off in a frenzy of desire, but she was disappointed that he had shown no interest at all.

Or was it relief?

"Hey! Isn't that the outfit you're working for?"

Harry's voice cut through her thoughts and she looked up. "What's that?"

"On the news—look—some talk about an American merger. That's the guy who owns CME. Piers Cordeaux. You ever met him?"

She looked at the little screen and felt her stomach tying itself in knots. There was Piers, cool, smiling, leaving his London headquarters and climbing into a large limousine, unruffled by the jostling reporters and flashlights.

"He came into the Filchester office once or twice."

"Too grand to notice a poor little student, eh?" he said, misreading her casual tone. "Lucky bastard. Bet with his money, he can have any woman he fancies."

Jez frowned. She wanted to say that Piers wasn't like that.

"Money doesn't get you everything, Harry."

"Don't you believe it!" He grinned at her, then turned back to the television.

§

They spent Christmas and New Year with Harry's parents at their big, rambling house in Waltham. Their stay was enlivened by visits from Harry's numerous brothers and sisters and their families, and they had to endure endless hints about more grandchildren and needing to settle down before they grew too old.

"Mum can't help it," said Harry, as they drove back to Luxbury through thick January fog. "She likes children."

"Well she should adopt some," snapped Jez, her temper worn thin by the visit. "And why does she have to keep on about us getting married?"

"She likes commitment."

"But we are committed! Just because we haven't made any final vows in a church doesn't mean we're not serious about this relationship."

"But it's not the same as getting married."

"Well it is to me," she said obstinately.

He glanced at her.

"I thought we agreed we didn't want commitment?" he countered. "After all, it was you who said we shouldn't tie ourselves down too young, because we still have our careers to sort out."

"Yes, but we've been together for nearly two years now. Commitment just builds up, bonds of trust and—and friendship."

She remembered the few days at the Manor with Piers. This was not a safe subject. What a hypocrite she was.

She was thankful to be back into the routine of working again after the Christmas break. She had found it very difficult to adjust to Harry being around again after living on her own for three weeks, so it was a relief to drive to CME.

Talk in the office centred on the proposed American deal.

"Do you think it will mean closure of this office?" said Melanie, who was busily painting each of her fingernails a different colour.

"I shouldn't think so. That's not the way Piers operates." Lavinia was calmly reassuring. "If he does a deal with the Americans it will be to bring *more* work here, not less."

Melanie held up one hand to study the effect of her multi-coloured fingers. "Oh, that's good. I really like it here, you know?"

"Yes, but that doesn't mean he'll keep on anyone not pulling their weight, Mel, and painting your nails is hardly productive, is it? Come on now, let's get back to work. Jessica. Can you give me a hand to finish this report, then we'll run through the first quarter's marketing campaign..."

§

The telephone was ringing as Jez opened the cottage door. She dashed to answer it.

"Hello? Oh, Harry. Hi."

"Sorry, love. I'm going to be late tonight. I've got to compile some data that needs to be ready by first thing tomorrow."

"Oh. I was hoping we could finish that fireplace tonight. There's not much time now before you go back to Cologne."

"I know love, and I'm sorry I haven't had much time to help you with it. But this is important—if I get this right, and they like my effort in Cologne, I'll be on my way with Tarrant International."

"You're right, but—oh Harry, I'm fed up with living in a mess!"

"Well, get someone in to finish it. It can't cost that much."

"No, I suppose not. I'll get the damp-proofing finished anyway, and get a quote from a builder for the rest." She tried to sound cheerful, determined not to whine. "So how late will you be?"

"I don't know. Very, I expect. You go on and eat and I'll grab something here."

Jez was too angry to eat. She pulled on Harry's old boiler-suit, tied back her hair and set to work on the remaining bricks in the fireplace. She had scarcely started when the doorbell rang. To avoid walking dust through the house she stepped out of her shoes and padded in her bare feet towards the door. Her irritation at this interruption evaporated when she saw her visitor.

"Kate! What are you doing here?"

"I had to go to Derby to visit a client, and as this is virtually on my way I thought I'd drop by. Have I caught you at a bad time?"

Jez grinned. She looked at Kate's immaculate pinstripe jacket and skirt, then glanced down at her own dusty coverall.

"Well, as long as you don't mind the mess—no. Have you time for a drink?"

"Coffee please, but have *you*? What are you doing?"

"Unblocking the old fireplace. Come and see."

"Can't you get someone in to do that?" Kate followed her to the back room, picking her way delicately over the dustsheets.

"Well we could, of course, but apart from the money, this is much more fun."

"Is it?"

"Well, no, not really, but you can work out an awful lot of aggression."

Kate looked at her. "Ah, I thought you sounded a bit tense. What's wrong. Harry?"

"Let's go into the kitchen. Yes, it is Harry, but it's not really his fault."

"It never is."

"Pardon?"

Kate shook her head. "Nothing. Carry on."

"Well, I had hoped he would help me with all this, but you know he was in Germany until Christmas, and he goes back there on the tenth. I was hoping I might go back with him for a few weeks but he says—well, I suppose it's hardly surprising that he's preoccupied. His job is really beginning to take off now, and I don't suppose I've been particularly attentive over Christmas." She spooned instant coffee into two mugs. "Is this okay? I've run out of the real thing."

"Yes, that's fine. Thanks." Kate took a mug, and Jez noted enviously the perfectly manicured nails. "So tell me, what happened to the rich guy who was chasing you?"

"Oh he's still around. He sent me flowers back in November," she said casually. "Oh, and he tried to give me a Porsche for Christmas." That cracked Kate's usually cool demeanour, and Jez laughed as her friend almost choked on her coffee. "It's true. He sent a Porsche round—luckily Harry was out so it was gone before he saw it—"

Kate was wide-eyed. "You mean you *turned it down*?"

"Of course. What else could I do?"

"I don't believe this. I think you dreamed the whole thing. No-one goes around giving away cars—and even fewer people refuse them!"

Jez shrugged.

"Well, it's true, Kate. And it's made it twice as difficult for me and Harry. I know how much his job means to him at the moment but I'm finding it really difficult to feel loving towards him. Maybe I'm trying to do too much, so there's not enough of me left for Harry..."

"Oh spare me the bleeding heart bit, Jez, I'm no good as an agony aunt. Look, when did you say Harry goes back to Germany? Why don't we go out for a meal that week, once he's gone? It might stop you feeling lonely, and we can have a good old gossip about men, life and the world in general. What do you say?"

"Great idea." The buzzing of the doorbell made her roll her eyes. "Busy night. Have a look on my calendar over there and pick a night while I answer the door."

Piers was leaning against the door post. "Hello Jez. Happy New Year."

Before Jez could think, he had stepped inside and was kissing her. It felt like the most natural thing in the world. He smelled of the cold, fresh night air but his lips were reassuringly warm, his tongue teasing and arousing all the sensations she had fought so hard to suppress.

She found herself revelling in the sensation for a brief moment before she forced herself to push him away. "What are you doing here?"

Their embrace had left him with a film of dust on the front of his jacket, but it didn't seem to bother him.

"I thought you might like to come out to dinner."

That made her laugh.

"Looking like this?" She glanced down at the dusty boiler-suit, several sizes too big for her and trailing on the floor around her feet.

"There's time for you to change."

"No, Piers. I'm waiting for Harry to come home."

"Then we'll get something delivered and we'll wait together."

"No!"

"Shall we shut the door?" he said, as if she had not spoken. "Your neighbours are getting curious."

Closing the door with Piers on the inside was a mistake, she decided, but she felt unequal to the struggle of forcibly ejecting him. She shut the front door and followed him into the lounge.

"Your jacket's covered in dust."

"It was worth it to kiss you."

She backed away. "Piers, you can't stay."

"Then come out with me."

"I can't, I'm working."

"You could stop working." He laughed. "You look like a Barbie doll in an action man suit!"

"Piers, it is *not* funny! Harry could be home at any minute."

"Ah, yes. Harry. What are we going to do about him?"

"Pardon?"

"Well, he is definitely a hindrance. You'd better tell him goodbye."

"Don't be ridiculous."

"I'm being deadly serious."

The laughter had gone from his face now, and she flushed at the look she encountered from his eyes.

"Harry and I are partners."

"So you've said." He reached out and slowly began to unzip the boiler-suit.

"Stop it."

"I thought you liked me undressing you."

Memories flared like a red-hot fire inside her. She felt her face burning and bit her lip, unable to meet his eyes. She turned away and zipped the coverall up to the neck.

"Piers, I—"

At that moment Kate appeared from the kitchen. Jez wondered if her face could burn any hotter without bursting into flames. By contrast, Piers looked totally unruffled. He smiled at Kate, who responded by stepping forward, holding out her hand.

"Hi. I'm Kate Hungerford, an old friend of Jessica's."

"Piers Cordeaux." Jessica bridled slightly as he gave Kate the full force of his charming smile. His gaze swept over her friend, taking in every well-groomed detail. "You don't look dressed for manual work, Kate…"

"No, I was just passing… I'm on my way back to Filchester. How about you?"

"Oh, I've an early appointment at the office tomorrow, so I'm staying over locally."

Jez shifted impatiently. "Look, if it's all the same to you, I want to get this finished…"

"Can I at least see what you're working on? Have you seen it, Kate?"

"Yes she's seen it. Look, Piers, I'll show you, if you promise to leave immediately after that." She led him to the doorway of the dining room. "I—*we*—are digging out the old fireplace."

Inside the room the dust hung in the air like fog. As they stepped into the room the wind sighed down the chimney, shifting the pattern of brick dust over the hearth.

"We're removing all the old bricks and rubble, then we'll clean it up and get the chimney unblocked. It'll give the room character."

While she was talking, Piers looked at the fireplace, running a hand over the exposed wooden beam.

"It's beautiful. You're right; it will make this a lovely room. So peaceful." He sighed. "I could be happy here."

She looked at him. "Why do you say that?"

"I don't know." He shrugged. "It's what I was thinking." He stood looking down at her. She could feel the tension between them. "Jez—"

A sudden fall of stones from the fireplace made her jump away, her heart hammering painfully against her ribs. "Oh my God—what am I doing? Piers, leave, please, now. Don't say anything, just go. Go!"

147

"Is that what you want?"

"It is. It *has* to be."

"Okay." He put a finger under her chin and forced her to look up at him. The mocking glint in his eyes faded when he saw the tears in her own. "Don't cry, love."

She tossed her head and sniffed. "I'm not."

"I'll ring you." He turned and walked out, calling goodbye to Kate as he passed the kitchen. A moment later she heard the front door slam.

Kate stood in the doorway, her eyes wide as she stared at Jez.

"My God—is that your millionaire?"

Kate's amazement made Jessica laugh, breaking the tension.

"Yes."

"Jessica, what are you doing throwing him out? He's drop-dead gorgeous!"

"I know—I mean—oh, you know what I mean."

"And he's clearly nuts about you."

"Is he?" Jez shook her head. "No, he's not. Look at me—a five-foot-four, short-sighted size fourteen with frizzy red hair. His girls are always tall, blond and beautiful." *A bit like you.*

"Oh Jez, don't be crazy. You're a size twelve and you look good in almost anything—except perhaps that stupid boiler-suit—and don't you dare call those pre-Raphaelite tresses of yours frizzy red hair—"

"Enough, Kate!" She put up her hand, laughing, "Anyway, I'm not his type. He's just huffy because I turned him down. If I gave in, he'd dump me in a week."

"Yeah, but what a week!" sighed Kate. "Did he say he'd call

you?"

"Uh-huh."

"Well, you're lucky to get another chance, girl."

"I don't *want* another chance. I'm happy with Harry."

Kate looked as if she would say more, but she merely shook her head and headed for the door. "Look, I've got to go, but you ring me if Harry, or this place or anything gets too much for you, promise?"

"I promise, Kate. And thanks."

Chapter Seventeen

"So you're a grass-widow again, Jessica. When did Harry leave?" Aunt Emmy handed Jez a cup of tea and came to sit beside her.

"Last Sunday."

"Missing him already? Is that why you've come to visit me?"

Jez merely smiled. Not for the world would she admit that she had felt only relief when they had parted. Their last few days had been marked by tension and ill temper. Harry had said goodbye to her with a tight little smile and a vague promise to call her.

"Never mind, darling. I'm glad you've come over here to see me. Now, what have you found out about Sarah and the cottage?"

Jez pulled out her notebook. "Not a lot, I'm afraid. The records for the cottage are incomplete. And there's nothing relevant until an entry in 1810, when the cottage was owned by a Phillipa Methven Grant. So there is probably some connection with Sarah Methven, but—"

"Wait a minute, dear!" Emmy hurried out of the room, to return a few moments later with a sheaf of papers. "Notes from my second visit to the church at Burford. I found a few more family references. Look, there's the entry for Sarah when she married Thomas Methven, and the two children are mentioned,

Thomas and Jennifer."

Jez found her excitement growing and she scanned the papers.

"And Jennifer married and had a daughter, another Jennifer, who married a Henry Grant—"

"And her daughter is Philippa Methven Grant. So we know how the family kept Lilac cottage. It was passed down through a female line. Now, what else did you learn?"

Jez smiled. "Aunt Emmy, you are insatiable. Well, I went to Luxbury church and found Sarah's grave."

"Oh, well done. And? Jez—what is it, what's the matter?"

"Probably nothing, but there was an old man in the churchyard. He—um—he told me some tale about his family being asked by Sarah's son to watch over the grave. He said that when Sarah was buried, a madwoman interrupted the service and tried to desecrate the grave. I think from what he said that it was the wife of Sarah's protector. Of course, he could have made it up. After all, he's talking about things that happened hundreds of years ago." She paused, picking at a loose thread in her skirt. "Emmy, do you believe in ghosts?"

"No, of course not."

Jez was reassured by this robust disclaimer and she smiled slightly. "The old man said there's a ghost comes to sit by Sarah's grave. He called him the duke."

"Sounds like he's a lonely old man who likes to talk."

"That's what the vicar said, but—it's a bit of a coincidence, isn't it?"

"No-o, it's the sort of story anyone could have made up."

"Could I have another look at the letters, Aunt Em?"

"Of course, but not tonight, love. You look worn out. You get a good night's sleep and I'll find the box for you in the morning."

Lying in bed later that night, Jez found thoughts of Piers and Harry threatened to crowd in on her and she was afraid she would not sleep, but gradually the peace of the little bungalow settled over her and she found herself drifting away...

§

"You are very quiet, my lady. The play did not please you?"

The carriage bumped and jolted over the cobbles.

"On the contrary, my lord. It pleased me very much, thank you."

"And the farce, you laughed at the farce?"

"I did, my lord."

"But now you are silent."

"Yes sir."

"Why should that be, madam? Does my company offend you?"

"No, sir. You are, as always, a most considerate host."

"And my friends, who came to speak with us?"

"They too, sir, were most courteous."

"Then what has overset you?"

"Nothing, my lord." She was grateful for the darkness, that the earl could not see her face.

"But it is so. I know your every mood, Sarah. Speak."

She drew a breath and sought for words that would not enrage him. "It—it is my situation that offends me, sir. I—I heard someone describe me tonight as—as your latest whore."

"Ignore them, Sarah. You are the envy of every woman—"

"No, sir. That I cannot allow."

"Well, of most women. Is that not sufficient?"

She did not answer, and heard him sigh with exasperation.

"Damme, madam, what do you want of me? I have given you everything but my name! You have every comfort, whatever little trinket your heart desires—is that not enough?"

"Not before God, my lord."

"Then God must—"

"Hush!" She leaned across and put her hand to his lips, horrified at his blasphemy. "Hush, sir. You must not endanger your soul further."

He caught her hand and kissed her fingers.

"My little angel." He laughed unsteadily and pulled her across onto his knees. "Your concern for my soul tells me you are not indifferent to me." She felt his hands stealing over her body and her senses stirred in response. He kissed her breasts, his breath warm on the white flesh. "Sarah. If this is sin, then devil take me, I'm a lost soul!"

She stroked his dark head.

"Pray do not say so, sir. Oh, Richard, Richard."

She sighed as she felt his hands pushing aside her heavy skirts, moving up over her thighs and exciting her very core. He lifted her from his knees and onto the carriage seat, kneeling before her and pushing himself between her thighs. She could not suppress a little gasp of pleasure, and he laughed again as he felt her succumb to desire.

"Sarah, *you* are my heaven!"

§

Jez woke with a start and lay still, wondering where she was. The dark room was unfamiliar. She knew she was on the edge of a dream, a confusing mix of pain and pleasure, while her eyes felt heavy, as if she had been crying. She stretched languorously, the way she did after making love. The memory was elusive, the more so as she tried to recapture it. Her nightdress was pulled up around her midriff. With a sudden shudder she wriggled to pull it down around her, even though she was still under the bedcovers.

At last Jez gave up her attempts to recapture her dream and went into the kitchen, where her aunt was already making tea.

"Good morning, Jessica. Did you sleep well?"

"Actually, no." Jez sat down at the little breakfast table. "Emmy, I think, I *think* I'm having dreams about Sarah. Her story seems so real to me, it's like I'm reliving it, as if she's haunting me—"

"You've been thinking too much about her, my love. Perhaps you should give it a break."

"Perhaps. But it's as if the story's inside me, but just out of reach of my consciousness. How can it be? I don't believe in ghosts, the supernatural and all that." She looked anxiously at the older woman. "Could there be something real, something physical passed down through the generations? Is that why I am so involved with Sarah?"

Emmy passed her niece a mug of tea and sat down opposite her.

"You mean like some sort of memory that's locked in the genes? No, Jez, I don't believe that's possible, and in any case it wouldn't make sense. Think it through, my dear. In order for what you are suggesting to happen, the memory would have to be Sarah's and passed on through Sarah's direct descendants.

You are related to her through an entirely different line. Besides, it would have to be through a child that she bore after she left her husband, and so far we have no record at all of any other children. I'll show you the family tree I've been working on—you'll see that I've traced our line of the family back to a James Appleton, Sarah's brother, so it would be impossible for you to be carrying a direct memory from Sarah, even if such a thing were possible."

"But it must be something, Auntie. I—I know so much more than the mere facts in the letters, and... I've had a couple of funny experiences."

"Tell me about them."

Jez sipped at her tea. She thought of lying in bed that morning. She could still feel the hands on her thighs, caressing her—she could hardly tell *that* to her aunt. Besides, it probably had more to do with Harry going away than anything supernatural.

"Well—nothing that I can really pinpoint, just dreams, sort of—you know, that feeling when you're not asleep, but not quite awake."

"Imagination," came the brisk reply. "You've been spending far too much time on your own, and that powerful imagination of yours is running away with you. You need to get out more with your friends."

"I did have dinner with Kate last week..."

"Good. Do it again."

Jez laughed.

"But seriously, Em, I'm busy all the time. I'm at CME for three days a week, I work at the Spinning Wheel two evenings, and the rest of the time I'm working on my thesis. And then there's the cottage to look after—the dining room's still not finished—I can't be *bored!*"

155

"No, but with Harry away, perhaps you're lonely."

"Perhaps." She finished her tea. "Aunt Emmy? Can I look at those letters again?"

"I thought we'd just agreed that you should let it rest."

"I can't Emmy, not yet. There's more I need to find out first. Please, Auntie."

Emmy was not impervious to her cajoling. With a shrug and a smile she capitulated.

"All right, my love, but do it early, then we can go for a walk and spend the evening talking about something entirely different, to take your mind off Sarah before bedtime."

Reading Sarah's journal for a second time, Jez found herself noticing the similarities between her present situation and Sarah's. They were both committed to one man before another, much richer one came on the scene. Perhaps, she thought slowly, perhaps Sarah's life was some sort of warning to her not to give in to Piers.

"There's a message here for me," she muttered, re-reading the letters. "She's telling me there's no happiness to be found that way."

Chapter Eighteen

A dry, cold February brought the promise of spring, and Jez worked with a vengeance, allowing herself no time to consider her situation with Harry or to think of Piers. She had not seen him since he had called at the cottage. He had not been to the Filchester office, but he phoned her every week. Each time he asked her to dinner and each time she refused. It had become a game, yet she found herself looking forward to his calls, deriving a guilty comfort from the knowledge that he still wanted her.

Her birthday brought a rash of cards from her family and friends and a huge spring bouquet from Piers. Harry's card arrived three days late, followed by an apologetic phone call, which incensed her so much that if Piers had phoned her then to invite her to dinner, she would have accepted. Unfortunately, Piers was unaware of her mood and it was almost a week before he rang her again.

"What are you doing on Saturday?"

"Decorating the dining room. The new plaster's dry, so I can paint it now."

"That can wait. You're coming out with me."

"I am not." She hoped he would argue, just so she could listen to his voice.

"My dear girl, what did you do on your birthday?"

"Nothing."

"Precisely. So look on it as a birthday treat."

"Thanks, Piers, but no thanks."

"May I ask why?"

"Because of Harry."

"Oh. And what do you think he is doing in Germany? Has it occurred to you that he might be enjoying himself in the evenings with a little female company?"

"No. I trust him." She frowned. He had spoiled the mood by making her think of Harry.

"You're a fool, Jez."

"I'd rather be a fool than a cheat!"

She slammed the phone down. Damn him! How dare he try to make her doubt Harry? A little voice in her head whispered that he might be right. After all, Harry's phone calls were less and less frequent, and he always sounded preoccupied, distant. Resolutely she pushed such thoughts out of her mind and went back to the coffee table, where her books and notes were strewn across the surface, but she could not settle. She prowled the empty house. Usually she was quite happy being alone, but now for the first time she found the emptiness unnerving.

"Don't be stupid," she told herself crossly. "You're letting him get to you. Stop it."

That weekend she pushed herself even harder, but her appearance the following Wednesday morning at the office caused even Lavinia to comment.

"I'm not ill, honestly." She laughed in answer to the marketing manager's concerned questioning. "I stayed up late last night to finish some decorating, that's all. I want to get the cottage tidy before Harry gets back, but it's been hard-going, and cleaning up the dust from the old fireplace has been very time-consuming—a bit like entering all these names on the database." She indicated the mailing list she was working on.

"Biggest problem with this new Knowledge Management System is that you have to accumulate the knowledge before you can manage it." Lavinia reached over and closed the folder. "Well, there's no hurry for that. Come and help me with my presentation. I haven't used that new software package as much as you, and you can help me put it all together."

"Great, anything to get away from data input. What's the presentation?"

"I've been invited to talk to the delegates from the Institute of Marketing. They're holding a seminar on Friday in Bromsgrove, and they want me to talk about marketing and the new technologies. Quite an honour, really."

"Wow, yes! Come on then, you give me the outline of what you're going to say, and we'll jot down some ideas."

"Good. And I need some captions for the display boards we're putting up. It's a big project, but good PR for CME, of course. Melanie's coming with me and we're going to set up the display tomorrow night and stop over at the hotel. Then on Friday she'll handle the computer projection for me, circulate the handouts and generally back me up—and I'll need it, I'm nervous already!"

But on Thursday Jez arrived to find the office in turmoil and Lavinia looking very harassed.

"Melanie's phoned in sick—she was dancing at some club last night and tripped over, wearing her new high platforms. She's broken her ankle."

"Oh, poor kid. But—your presentation—"

"I know! We were going to leave straight from work tonight, but she says they won't let her out of hospital until tomorrow at the earliest—complications with the break, or something. I suppose I'll have to go alone, unless—" She looked at Jez, a hopeful gleam in her eye. "Would *you* come with me Jessica? You've worked on the script, so you know the cues."

"Me? What about the others in the office?"

"None of them know this computer package as you do. Could you do it, Jez, please? Unless, of course, you have other plans for tonight?"

Jez thought of the empty house. She had planned to finish clearing up after her blitz on the dining room, but that held very little appeal.

"No, I'm not doing anything, Vinnie, but I'll have to get an overnight bag."

"That's no problem." Lavinia was too relieved to have a replacement for Melanie to worry over detail. "We'll run through everything here and pack it all away, then you can go home and pack and I'll pick you up about five. How's that?"

"Fine." Jez gave a shaky laugh. "I just feel like I've been steamrollered."

§

The conference organiser, a senior member of the Institute of Marketing, stood at the front of the room, waiting for the last of the delegates to take their seats. She looked the epitome of the successful businesswoman, with her short dark hair and impeccably tailored suit of apricot wool. When everyone was seated, she began to speak in a clear, well-modulated tone that was obviously used to command. "Well, good morning everyone. I am glad you could all make it, and on such a bitterly cold day, too. We have a packed programme for you today. Later we have the marketing manager from CME, a young company with an impressive track record..."

Jez sat beside Lavinia in one corner of the conference room, a thick wad of notes on the table before her. Lavinia's talk was to be the final one of the afternoon, and despite her nervousness at the approaching ordeal, Jez found the morning speakers both interesting and entertaining. When the meeting adjourned for lunch, Lavinia scribbled furiously on her notepad.

"They were so good they've given me a few ideas for this afternoon," she explained, her pen flying over the page. "There. That's it. Come on then, Jessica, let's get some lunch."

"Lavinia Woods. Wondered when I saw the name on the programme if it would be you."

Lavinia turned in her chair to stare up at the tall angular man standing over her, and a delighted smile spread slowly over her face.

"James! How great to see you!" She stood up and kissed him, laughing and talking at the same time. "How are you? It must be—wait...it must be all of three years."

Smiling, Jez tried to slip away but Lavinia caught her arm.

"Jez, don't go. Let me introduce you. This is James Hartley-Paige, an old friend of mine. James—Jessica Skelton, my assistant for the day."

James held out his hand, smiling warmly.

"Jessica. Have you worked long with Lavinia? A hard taskmaster, isn't she?"

"Oh, you! You make me sound like an ogre. We should go and get some lunch before it's too late. Come on, Jez."

"You go on. I just want to run through things here once more to check everything's working." She smiled. "Go on, you two. Don't worry about me, I had a huge breakfast."

Jez watched as they strolled out of the room, absorbed in

each other, then with a faint sigh she settled down to check through her notes. It was almost an hour later when the delegates filed back into the conference room. Lavinia and James Hartley-Paige were still talking. At last they separated and Lavinia came over to join her.

"Are we all set? God, I'm nervous."

"Don't worry, you'll be fine once you get started."

"I know, I just hate the build-up. I—oh, God!"

"Now what's wrong?"

Lavinia was staring towards the door and Jez followed her gaze. Piers was standing in the doorway, smiling and turning his powerful charm on the conference organiser, who was beaming up at him, quite enchanted. Jez could imagine his words: *I am sorry, I haven't been invited...I just wondered if you could find room for me...* They would let him in, of course. What a coup to have the rich and famous Piers Cordeaux at your seminar. As he walked across the room towards them she schooled her features into what she hoped was a cool but friendly smile, but her heart was hammering so hard against her ribs she could hardly breathe, and she leaned against the table, afraid that her wayward legs would not support her.

"Hi." He smiled at them both, then leaned forward to kiss Lavinia.

Jez kept her attention firmly on her notes, her body language shouting at him to keep away. Lavinia was almost cooing with delight.

"Piers! What on earth are you doing here?"

"I'd half-planned to take a day off when I remembered you had this conference coming up. Thought I'd drop by to watch your performance. Hope you don't mind?"

"No, no, of course not. But I'm really nervous—forgive me if

I make a few mistakes."

"You'll be fine, I know it. I'll just sit here by Jez. Go on now, and don't worry, they won't bite you!"

The noise in the room subsided as the organiser took the stage and they sat down as she ran through the itinerary for the afternoon session.

Lavinia's presentation was flawless. Jez forced herself to concentrate on the cues for changes to the images on the big wall-screen, although she never quite forgot that Piers was sitting beside her. The presentation lasted exactly forty minutes. Lavinia finished her summing up, and under cover of the ensuing applause Piers leaned across to Jessica.

"What are you doing here? I thought Melanie was helping on this."

"She's broken her ankle, so I stepped in."

"That was good of you. I'll bet Vinnie was relieved."

Jez thawed enough to grin at him. "She freaked out at the thought of doing this on her own."

"I can imagine. Looks like the conference is over. Let me give you a hand to clear this away."

The delegates were drifting into the anteroom for coffee before departing and, after they had packed away the computer and sales aids, Jessica and Piers followed them. Jez spotted Lavinia with James Hartley-Paige.

"Do you know the man talking to Vinnie?" she asked as they approached the couple.

"You mean Hartley-Paige?" Piers lowered his voice. "He and Vinnie used to be an item a few years ago, but he was going through a particularly messy divorce at the time, so Vinnie stepped back, said they both needed some space." He smiled as they came up to Lavinia and her companion. "Hi Jim, nice to see you again. How's business—got your own agency in Birmingham now, haven't you?"

"Mm, doing well, too. You should try us sometime."

"Maybe I will. Well done, Vinnie. Excellent presentation."

"Thanks, Piers—and thank you, Jessica, for coming along at such short notice. I don't know what I would have done without you."

Jez felt her cheeks burning, especially with Piers smiling down at her. She excused herself to collect a cup of coffee, and when she came back she heard James talking to Lavinia.

"Look, I've a contact at the Symphony Hall who can always pick up tickets. How about I get a couple for tonight? It's Mozart, the clarinet concerto, I think. You were always fond of Mozart. We could get a meal somewhere, and you could stay over and drive back tomorrow."

"Oh Jim, I'd love to, but Jez and I came together, you see, and—"

Jez shook her head. "That's no problem, Lavinia. You could drop me at the station and I'll take a train back—"

"Oh no, Jez, I couldn't let you do that," cried Lavinia.

"No need. I'll drop Jez home."

Piers' smooth tones interjected and Jez almost choked on her coffee. She looked up, about to protest, but the words died on her lips when she saw the relief on Lavinia's face and realised how much she wanted to spend the evening with her old flame.

Lavinia turned towards Jez. "Will that be all right? You're sure it's okay, Jessica?"

"Of course, if Piers doesn't mind." She seemed to have no

control over her words.

"Not at all. It will be a pleasure."

"That's great! Thank you, Piers. Look, Jez, you can leave all the display boards and things—Jim and I will pack them into my car."

"Fine." Piers looked at his watch. "It's past five, shall we get moving, Jez? Have you much luggage to collect?"

Jez tried to concentrate. Events were overtaking her again. "Mm? Oh—yes—I mean no. Only a small bag. I'll get it now."

She wanted to protest, to say she would much rather take a train than go with Piers, but it was impossible. Lavinia's grateful look when they said goodbye was some measure of consolation.

As they left the hotel it was beginning to snow, little icy flakes coating the roads and cars.

Jez buttoned her coat. "You know I only agreed to this for Vinnie's sake."

"Very noble of you."

Jez bit her lip. A dignified silence was her best hope. She followed Piers across the well-lit car park to a long-nosed sports car. As he stowed away her luggage in the boot she caught a glimpse of the distinctive Aston Martin badge.

"Another company car?"

"Oh, no. This one's all mine." He held open the door for her.

"Why don't you choose a sensible motor, like a four-wheel drive," she muttered, casting a doubtful glance at the fine covering of snow on the road.

"It happened to be a clear sky when I left London this morning." He closed the door with rather more force than was necessary.

165

"You can always drop me at the station."

The powerful engine roared into life.

"No. I promised Vinnie I'd take you home."

"Thank you. I'm very grateful."

He laughed at that, his ill humour forgotten.

"No, you're not! You're angry because you've been outmanoeuvred."

"You're right," she admitted, "and I can't even blame you for it."

"No, I'm as much a victim of fortune as you this time." He glanced across at her, a smile lifting the corners of his mouth. "Truce?"

"Truce." She settled back into the comfortable leather seat and relaxed, too tired to fight.

Chapter Nineteen

The volume of traffic in the town was keeping the roads clear, but by the time they reached the motorway it was snowing hard, thick flakes flying towards them and building into a white frame on the edges of the windscreen. The traffic slowed to a crawl. Piers tuned the radio to the traffic reports.

"Heavy snow falling in the Midlands... M69 closed north of Coventry... M1 closed north of junction 20... A46 southbound blocked by a jack-knifed lorry...motorists are advised to avoid the area for the next few hours..."

"Sounds as if everything's coming to a standstill." Piers leaned forward, staring out at the swirling snow which was now beginning to coat the road signs. "We're approaching a junction. I think we should get off the motorway while we can. We could be snarled up in traffic for hours. What do you think?"

"Whatever you say—I don't know this area very well."

He pulled onto a slip road and headed off the motorway.

Jez peered out the window. "Where are we going?"

Piers did not answer immediately, for the car hit a patch of ice and he fought to stop it careering into the bank. Not wanting to distract him, she did not repeat her question. As they drove away from the motorway, the roads were almost deserted and soon they were driving through an unfamiliar white landscape.

"I'm heading for the Manor. It's only a few miles from here, and I think we should get off the road until the weather improves."

She stared at the white verges, where the snow was piling up. "No chance of that for a while, I think."

Piers turned on the radio again, but the weather reports were not encouraging. Snow was forecast for several hours, strong north easterly winds, drifting. Jez kept her eyes fixed on the snow-covered road and wondered how Piers could find his way. The sports car slewed occasionally on the slippery roads, and she reluctantly admired his skill in keeping the powerful engine in check. The snow was building up on the road itself, forming deep drifts against any obstacle. She began to fear that the low Aston Martin would soon find it impossible to get through.

"Here we are."

She looked up and saw the lights of the Manor shining through the trees ahead of them. They slid into the drive and crawled towards the hotel.

"Shall I drop you at the door?"

"No, let's park and I'll walk back with you—if you stop on this you might not get going again."

Once they had parked, Jez climbed out of the car and pulled up her collar against the biting wind. Piers hooked his small overnight bag on his shoulder and picked up her holdall, then they set off towards the welcoming lights of the entrance. Her heels slipped on the icy ground and she instinctively put out her hand. Piers took her arm and walked her quickly across to the entrance. As they entered the hotel she felt her face glowing in the sudden heat. He put down the bags, grinning at her as he pulled off his gloves.

"I didn't like to say anything back there, but we came very

close to getting stuck a couple of times."

"I know. And I was beginning to think we were lost. I didn't see a road sign for miles. Lucky you know this road so well."

"Come on, let's get cleaned up." He lifted an eyebrow. "One room or two?"

"Two," she said firmly.

She watched as he spoke to the receptionist. She felt an almost physical blow as she realised again just how attractive he was. His black hair was gleaming with melted snow and the turned-up collar of his dark coat gave him the look of an adventurer. A buccaneer, she thought, or latter-day pirate...

Down, girl! she told herself. *You're on dangerous ground.* She hoped Piers could not read her thoughts as he turned to speak to her.

"Do you mind a room in the old wing? It's all they have left."

The receptionist was eager to explain. "A lot of our guests should have been leaving tonight but unfortunately, due to the snow, they can't get away..."

"No, no, that will be fine. I was in the old part of the house last time—" she broke off, blushing, and was grateful that Piers appeared not to notice.

He picked up her bag, glancing at her key. "Room forty-six. Come on then, I'll drop you off. My suite is at the end of that corridor."

"Hang on—if they're so busy, how did *you* manage to get a suite?"

He grinned and leaned closer to say quietly, "I told you, I own the place. Come on."

When they reached room forty-six he unlocked the door and carried her bag into the room.

"Hmm, a bit small—are you sure you don't want to share mine?"

"It's fine." She took her bag and gave him a push towards the door. "Go and have a cold shower, Piers."

He grinned. "I've booked dinner for nine, that suit you? Good. I'll call for you at eight thirty."

Jez shut the door, smiling. How easily they slipped into this bantering. He found her attractive and it showed—she might not be able to reciprocate, but she was human enough to be flattered. She thought of him now as a friend, and as long as the banter did not get out of hand she could relax in his company.

She glanced at her watch: time for a shower and a change of clothes. The little bathroom was cramped, the obligatory en-suite built into the bedroom. This was obviously one of the smaller rooms, used only when everything else had been taken. The wall panelling was probably original and the faded velvet drapes were in need of replacing. Even the lighting was substandard, with the lights by the bed and over the mirror not working at all. She grinned. She'd complain to the management—better still, the owner.

After showering, Jez pulled on the heavy towelling bathrobe she found hanging on the bathroom door. She took off the shower cap and shook out her hair. It was still damp from the snow and curled wildly about her head. She suddenly remembered Kate's comment about pre-Raphaelite tresses— perhaps she would drag a comb through it and leave it loose tonight.

Jez yawned, suddenly feeling very tired. It had been a very long day. She walked to the window to pull the curtains but stood for a moment, her head resting against the wooden frame, watching the snow. It was still falling heavily, large feathery flakes hurtling against the window before being whipped away by the blustery wind that moaned around the old building. The movement was relaxing, mesmerising.

Suddenly, Jez was aware that she was not alone. Someone was behind her, very close, and the subtle smell of sandalwood filled her senses. A hand stole around her waist.

"Oh Piers, I thought we had agreed." She could not resist him. With her eyes still closed, she tilted her head back, silently willing him to kiss her neck. His lips were gentle on her skin, the merest touch. The bathrobe fell open and she gave a long, shuddering sigh as his hand moved up to caress her breasts.

"No, no don't."

"You know you want me." The words were a whisper, almost inaudible, close to her ear. "Don't fight me, I'll never let you go now. Ah, Sarah, Sarah."

Jez started. She opened her eyes and for a moment stood rigid, a cold chill running down her spine.

"Piers?" She forced herself to turn around.

The room was empty.

She pulled the bathrobe around her and tied the belt in a knot, trying to control the shivering.

"Where are you? *Who* are you?" she whispered, her eyes straining to pick out the slightest movement, the faintest shadow.

The room was empty, but she did not *feel* alone. Her words echoed around the room, unnaturally loud, bouncing off the panelled walls. She slumped on the bed and reached for the telephone. Dead. Jez forced her trembling legs to move and stumbled to the door, but it resisted her attempts to open it. She took a deep breath. She must not panic. She dare not lose control. Slowly she tried the door again, but still it would not open.

"This fear is in *me*," she said aloud. "This is my imagination. There is nothing to be afraid of."

"Sarah."

Had she heard it? Perhaps it was just the wind outside. She felt a draught on her face, as though something had come close, disturbing the air around her. Suddenly she wanted to be out of that room. She banged on the door with her fists.

"Help! Anyone—help!" She hammered and kicked the door, screaming. In her distress she did not hear the footsteps in the corridor, or the voices.

"Someone in that room, sir? Yes, I've a master key—but it's not locked. I can't open it, they must be leaning against the door—"

"Jez? Move away from the door. Jez—"

She was crouched against the door, sobbing with fear. Someone was pushing at the door, trying to get into the room.

"Jez, we can't open the door unless you move away. Move back."

She shifted slightly and the door opened wider, enough for someone to enter. Piers was the first through the gap, dragging her out of the way to allow two hotel porters to follow him. They stood in the doorway, looking anxiously down at her.

After a quick glance around the room, Piers nodded at them. "It's all right. I'll handle this now. Thanks."

The men hovered, looking concerned. "Perhaps we should get a doctor..."

Kneeling beside Jessica, he shook his head impatiently.

"Do you think you'll get anyone to come out in this weather? She's fainted, that's all. I'll take care of her. You can go." He waited until they had left the room, then said softly, "Jez. Jez, it's all right, I'm here. Come on now." He lifted her to her feet.

"There was someone here—I thought it was... He t-touched me, c-couldn't open the door—" She was shaking uncontrollably.

"No-one's here, love, only me."

She stared at him for a long time, unable to focus. Then gradually recognition returned and she clung to him, sobbing.

Piers held her until the tears subsided into the occasional hiccough, and when Jessica wanted to move away he made no move to restrain her.

"I—um—I must have fainted. I haven't eaten anything since breakfast."

"You'll feel better when you've had some food—or would you rather sleep for a bit?"

"No, don't leave me! I mean—Piers—there *was* someone, something in this room."

"Jez, it was a nightmare."

She shrugged, the terror fading now she was not alone.

"Well, whatever it was, it scared me." She looked at him, then down at her hands, her fingers nervously twisting the ties from her bathrobe. "I know it's stupid—and please don't take this the wrong way! But, I—I don't want to be alone."

He didn't laugh.

"Why don't you get dressed and come up to my suite? I'll order dinner to be sent up to us. No tricks. I promise I won't jump on you. Come on, Jez. You can trust me."

Her smile was perfunctory. "All right. Thanks."

Piers ordered dinner while she dressed and packed her bag. She paused. Surely, the telephone had not worked when she tried it earlier?

Piers led her to the private suite at the end of the corridor. For a moment she forgot her fears as she took in the size of the apartment. The large lounge included a huge square bay window, hung with rich blue drapes that shut out the wintry night. Through an open door she glimpsed the bedroom, complete with a heavily carved four-poster.

"Wow, you get this suite every time?"

He nodded solemnly. "One of the perks of being in the trade."

She sank into the cushions on one of the large sofas. "This is nice—comfortable."

"Can I get you a drink? There's a bar—"

"No, I'd rather not—unless you have some tea?"

"Tea it is." He tossed the TV handset to her. "Why don't you check out the weather?"

She flicked through the channels and found the local news.

"Doesn't look good," she said when he handed her a cup. "The whole area has come to a standstill. And they're forecasting even more snow overnight."

He sat down beside her.

"Looks like we're here for the night then." The TV screen showed lines of snow-covered cars stopped on the motorway. "Lucky we turned off when we did."

Jez sipped her tea and frowned.

"Piers? Why do you always make me Earl Grey?"

"I don't know. I thought you liked it."

"I do, but I didn't *know* I liked it until you made it for me."

She blushed. "The last time we were here."

He grinned. "Association of ideas. Makes you remember a pleasurable event."

That drew a smile from her, but it was short-lived.

"I can't explain it, but something weird happened to me tonight. It scared me."

"You had a nightmare, that's all."

"You don't have nightmares standing up," she objected. "And it was so real." She shuddered. "I can feel his hands on me, even now."

Piers took the cup from her shaking hands.

"Hush, Jez. It's all right." He put his arms round her and cradled her head against his shoulder. Gradually the tension left her body and she relaxed against him.

"Piers? I—I think I'm being haunted." She waited for him to laugh, to make a joke, but he merely held her tighter.

"Tell me about it."

And gradually, she told him about Sarah, the discovery of her journal and the letters. "I think it's Sarah's lover who is haunting me."

"Very likely, in your mind. You're so involved with this Sarah person that you've become obsessed with this lover of hers."

"But I haven't. I know I haven't!"

"And perhaps it's tied up in some deep psychological way with your own love-life problems." He saw that she was about to protest and put up a hand. "Okay, okay, I won't say anymore."

There was knock at the door. "Room service, sir."

"Good. Dinner at last." He got up. "No, no, you stay there and I'll bring it to you."

Jez curled up on the sofa and allowed Piers to wait on her. There was smoked salmon and wafer-thin brown bread, succulent chicken cooked in wine and a bottle of chilled white Burgundy that he persuaded her to try. She sipped at her wine, relaxing a little. The memory of her nightmare was gradually fading, yet even when she was talking to Piers, she remained alert, her eyes darting to the corners of the room, watching the shadows.

"What's wrong Jez?"

"I feel as if someone's watching us. He's in the shadows, in the very fabric of the building."

"He?"

She shrugged. "I know it's a man."

"It's your imagination Jez. Come on, you told me you'd read philosophy, use it now. Logical argument. Explain to yourself what's happening."

She was silent, thinking of her meeting with old Tom at the churchyard. It could all be explained, of course. Coincidence, imagination. Yet there was something else, some stirring of images at the very edge of her memory.

"Do you think I'm having a breakdown?"

He laughed. "No, but I think perhaps your brain's gone into overdrive. You need to relax." He used the handset to select the built-in audio system. "What would you like, pop, classical?"

"I don't mind. You choose." She leaned back and closed her eyes as the music began. "What's this?"

"Handel. Don't you like it?"

"Yes, I do."

"Good. You relax. I've got to make some calls, but I'll do it from the bedroom so I don't disturb you."

"Thanks." She stretched out on the sofa, her eyes closed,

and let her mind drift.

§

Sarah was sitting before the dressing table, staring at her reflection in the mirror. Her eyes looked large, a deep luminous green in the light of the candles, their colour enhanced by the whiteness of her painted skin. The candles flickered as the door opened behind her, and the strains of music from the ballroom became momentarily louder.

"Sarah, will you not come downstairs? I gave this ball in your honour, to show you off to my Warwickshire neighbours."

"No, my lord. They despise me."

"That is untrue. One ill-judged remark at dinner—"

"They are laughing up their sleeves at me."

"Nonsense. You imagine it, Sarah. They do not dare offend me."

"No, but they know I am your whore."

"You will not use that word!"

She blinked rapidly.

"'Tis but the truth, sir."

He went down on his knees beside her, catching her hands.

"Sarah, Sarah my love. Pray do not torture me with your moralising. You know I would make you my wife an I could, but even if Parliament granted me a divorce there is your own husband—"

"There is only one solution to this, Richard. You must let me go."

"Never."

She gazed at him, pleading with him to understand. "Can you not see, my dear lord, the longer you keep me with you, the more you sin against God?"

"So you would leave me, destroy my happiness."

I would give my very life for your happiness an it did not endanger your soul. She looked away, that he might not read the message in her eyes.

"I would have you at your peace with your Maker, sir."

"There is time yet to repent. Now, my lady, is the time to dance." Lord Cordeaux rose to his feet and held out his hand imperiously. "Come. You will grace my party with your presence. I command it."

"As you wish, sir."

Fixing her smile, Sarah accompanied the earl to the ballroom. Under Lord Cordeaux's watchful eye, she danced and smiled throughout the night. Her reserve and gentle manners puzzled those who knew the earl well—this lady was very different from his usual mistresses. They whispered to themselves, never before had Cordeaux brought a mistress into Warwickshire. Was the rakish earl tamed at last? And what of his long-suffering wife? It was common knowledge she had lovers of her own, and the earl made her a generous allowance, so, they reasoned, everyone was happy.

They did not get to bed until the sun was rising and the earl, delighted with the success of the ball, was only too eager to share his pleasure with his lady. For Sarah, tired and distressed by the role she had been forced to play, this conclusion of the night's activities was but one more trial. Thomas had never expected her to enjoy his attentions, but he was her husband, and she had forced herself to endure them in silence. Now, when her body ached to respond to the earl's lovemaking, she forced herself to remain passive, convinced that any admission of her love for Cordeaux would ensure their eternal damnation.

Chapter Twenty

Jez woke up to find bright sunlight streaming into room. She was still lying on the sofa, but she was now covered by a warm rug. She stirred and Piers stepped into view. He was already dressed and he dropped down to sit on the edge of the sofa.

"So you're awake." He gently smoothed a strand of red hair away from her face.

"Have I been here all night?"

"You have. I was going to offer you the bed after I'd finished my calls but when I came back you were asleep. You looked so comfortable I didn't like to disturb you."

She sat up and stretched. "What time is it?"

"Nine. Why don't you freshen up and we'll get some breakfast? You can use the bedroom—promise I won't come in."

He rose and held out his hand to help her to her feet.

"Thanks." She stopped as she passed him, looking up shyly. "Thanks for everything, Piers. You've been a real friend."

He stared down at her for a moment, a look in his eyes that she could not understand. He gave her a wry smile and shook his head.

"Oh no, love. I'm not your friend. I still want you, and I'm not giving up. But last night we called a truce, remember?"

"I remember."

"And that ends as soon as I've delivered you to your door. Now go and get yourself ready so we can have breakfast."

They drove away from the Manor under an unbroken blue sky, with only the black lines of the cleared roads cutting through the dazzling white landscape. As they sped towards Filchester Jez tried to think through the night's events.

"I still can't explain what happened in room forty-six. I'm sorry."

"It's okay. You had a panic attack. It happens."

"Not to me."

"Jez?"

"Yes?"

"Who's Richard?"

"Richard?"

"Yes. When we got to your door you were calling for Richard. Who is he? Some old boyfriend?"

She frowned.

"No, I don't know anyone called Richard."

"You said his name again in your sleep this morning."

She shrugged. "Just something else I can't explain."

They did not speak again until Piers turned into Luxbury High Street. "Will you be all right—on your own, I mean?"

"Of course."

He drew the car to a halt outside the cottage.

"Thanks for the lift."

"No problem." He took her hand. "Are you sure you don't want me to come in with you?"

"Certain." She tried a smile. "I think my resolve to keep you at arm's length would weaken if you did."

"That's what I'm hoping for."

"No, Piers, I can't."

He squeezed her hand and let it go. "Go on then. And if you can't make work on Monday, don't worry. I'll sign your sick note."

"Are you joking?" She rallied bravely. "I have to be in or Vinnie will skin me alive."

Alone in the cottage, Jez wandered restlessly through each room, trying to put her jumbled thoughts in order. She made herself a coffee and went back to the dining room. She had painted the walls in cream and touches of deep red, but even with the sun streaming through the window the room felt cold. She stared at the newly opened hearth. There was a fireplace shop in Filchester. She would contact them and ask them to fit a fire basket and check the chimney. Then she would buy a few logs and some coal and have a real fire burning there when Harry got back. Harry.

"Oh Harry, come home!"

There was no reply from Harry's number in Germany. With a sigh Jez switched on the television, but after flicking through the channels two or three times she gave up. She should try to work out just what was happening to her, but part of her shied away from the confrontation, especially alone. Desperate to talk to someone, she tried Kate's mobile, but only the answerphone responded. She flicked through her address book and stopped at a number she had rarely used. Her fingers trembled slightly as she keyed in the numbers.

"Hello Mum."

"Hi darling! How are you? It's such a long, long time since we spoke. How are you?"

"Not bad. Mum—"

"And how's Harry?"

"He's fine. He's in Germany at the moment, that's why I called—"

"Oh darling, such a bore for you to be on your own."

"It is. I—I wondered if I could fly out and see you."

"Darling, that would be wonderful. I thought you would never—I mean, I know how difficult it has been for you to accept Bruno. You'd love Puerto Banus, and you'd be more than welcome here, only Bruno and I are off to Mexico at the end of the week. What dreadful timing. How long is Harry away for? If it's going to be for months we'll be back in four weeks..."

"No, no. It doesn't matter."

"You could both come, when Harry gets home. How would that be, come and get some sun. I bet it's raining there, isn't it?"

Jez glanced out the window.

"It's been snowing, actually, but that's not important."

"Jez, darling—is anything wrong?"

Her mother's voice held a note of concern and she hesitated. What could she say—yes, everything's wrong! My boss wants to get me into bed and I'm being haunted by a three-hundred-year-old ghost?

"No, Mum. I'm just a bit down because Harry's away."

"Don't you have any friends who could come and stay?"

Jez laughed at that.

"Oh, Mum. You make it sound like I'm fourteen, not twenty-four. Don't worry, I'll be fine. By the way, do you know any family history, I mean *old* family history, like one of our ancestors running away from her husband?"

"What an odd question! No-o, I don't think so. We've always been a very boring family—pillars of society and all that. When I wanted to divorce your father to marry Bruno it caused quite a stir, but your Nan and Pops were alive then and they believed in marriage at all costs. That's why I stuck it out. Then, when your father died...but by then of course your grandparents were no longer around—heaven knows what they would have said about you and Harry living together."

"You don't have to be married to be faithful, Mum."

"Oh, I know, dear, I know... Heavens, is that the time? Must fly, love. One of Bruno's clients has just arrived in town, there's a champagne reception on his yacht and I haven't even changed yet."

"Okay, Mum."

"Jessica! You will ring again, won't you darling?"

"Of course. Have a great holiday and I'll talk to you when you get back. Say hello to Bruno for me. 'Bye..."

Jez replaced the receiver, feeling more alone than ever. The silence in the cottage closed around her, almost overwhelming her with its heaviness. She reached for the telephone again. It rang for a long time before she heard her aunt's voice crackling in her ear.

"Jez! How nice—sorry darling, can't stop now. I have a taxi at the door. I'm off to London for a few days."

"Oh."

"Yes. Going to see an old friend of mine. Could be useful."

"But Emmy, I have to talk to you—"

"Yes love, that would be very nice. Let me see, why don't you come down next weekend?"

"Next—yes, yes. All right."

"Good. That's settled then, and I might even have more

news for you, about Sarah, I mean. Oh heavens, the taxi! Must dash, love. 'Bye!"

Jez shook her head, smiling despite the misery inside her. She felt swept along by her aunt's enthusiasm. She hadn't even found out why Emmy was going to London.

Chapter Twenty-one

London. It was a strange quirk of fate that saw Jez herself on the train to London later that week. A memo had arrived for Lavinia from Piers, suggesting that Jez might like to spend a day at Cordeaux House, the headquarters of CME.

"It's almost a command." Vinnie had smiled. "I suppose it's my fault really. I told him that I wanted you to join the team working with the advertising agency from next Monday, putting the promotion schedule together for the new Sentinel software. Piers probably thought it would be a good thing to get the London trip out of the way before getting tied up in Sentinel. So, is that okay with you, Jez?"

"Y-yes, I suppose so."

Jez arrived at CME's head office in Kensington mid-morning. She stood for a moment at the entrance, looking up at the building. A chill breeze made her shiver despite the warm April sunshine. Cordeaux House was a large Georgian building in warm red brick fronted by a creamy portico supported on four Ionic pillars. The tall metal gates were pushed back to each side of the wide drive. She stepped forward and gave her name to the security guard in his small kiosk. He checked his list of visitors and waved her in the direction of the curving gravelled drive that led to the front of the house. The large double doors of the entrance stood open and she went into the marbled hall. A modern lift had been built at one side, and directly in front of her was a huge glass wall with automatic doors in the centre leading to the reception and office area. As she approached the doors they slid open with a whisper.

Sarah.

Jez reported to reception and a few moments later a tall blond woman in a pale grey trouser suit came down the sweeping staircase and approached her with a smile.

"Hi. I'm Drina McIntosh. I run the operation here in London for Piers. He told me you were coming today. First of all let me give you one of these. It's a security pass card. Swipe it through the sensor boxes by the lift or the main doors and they will open for you. It's only valid inside the building—you would need to know the keypad combination as well as having one of these to get in from outside. Now, let me show you around..."

"She's here."

"Who?"

"Jessica Skelton." Drina McIntosh put a sheaf of papers on Piers' desk. "Very attractive too. Latest conquest?"

Piers put down his pen and sat back. "Why, do you fancy her yourself?"

"No point if she has the hots for you."

"That's just it. She's not interested."

Drina smiled.

"Oh-ho! New experience for you, Piers. A woman who can resist your charms."

"You always have."

"Guys aren't my scene. I'm talking about red-blooded heterosexual women. And anyway," she added, "I *do* find you

187

very charming, even if I don't want to jump into bed with you."

He laughed.

"Thanks, Drina! Praise indeed. Look after her for me, give her lunch and all that. I'll say hello to her later."

Piers kept himself busy until three o'clock, then he gave in to temptation and went in search of Jez. He found her in accounts and noted she was wearing a slate grey suit with a short skirt that made the most of her marvellous legs. They shook hands and he kept his greeting formal, knowing anything else and she would shy away like a frightened filly.

"So, have you had a good day?"

"Yes, thank you. Very informative, and it's a beautiful building. But isn't it expensive?"

"It is, but a London address is always useful." He added, casually, "Not only that, it's my ancestral home."

"Oh. I thought you named it Cordeaux House when you bought it."

"It was built in the early eighteenth century by the fourth Earl of Cordeaux. You probably noticed that the pediment is engraved with the date 1790, but that was added by a later earl. The main building was finished in 1746." Unable to resist, he murmured, "Which coincidentally is the code I use for the security keypad to the building, just in case you want to sneak back in and see me tonight."

She could not resist an answering grin. "No, thanks."

"Oh well, it was worth a try. Let's get back to business. How much has Drina shown you?"

"All the main offices on the ground floor."

"Would you like to see the rest of the building?"

"Yes, please—if you have time."

"Sure. Come on." He led her up the wide staircase. "The house passed out of my family before the war and since then it has had a chequered history, but luckily it's never been turned into apartments. It was in a pretty poor state when I bought it three years ago, but we've kept as many of the original features as we could."

They reached the main landing and he pointed to a second flight of stairs. "That leads to a few smaller offices and store rooms. The roof had fallen in and everything upstairs has had to be renewed, so there's very little of interest there, I'm afraid, but on this floor we've kept the main apartments very much as they have always been. You probably know that they used to build these places with one room leading from another, no corridors. We've tried to keep it like that. This is the boardroom—used to be the grand salon, for balls and assemblies, things like that."

"It's beautiful. And the chandeliers, did you have to buy those?"

"No. We found them in one of the attics. Of course they are never used now. I've put in modern lighting and extra wall lamps. We've also a few good paintings for the walls, Turner, Rembrandt, Gainsborough—copies, of course, but they impress the Americans. I have a couple of originals for my office."

Jessica ran her hand along the oak panelling. "It's a beautiful house. I love these carvings."

"A thousand thanks, madam."

She laughed at the old-fashioned words, her eyes taking in the detail of the intricate carving. "You're welcome. But I hope you have more heating on in here when you have your meetings. I wouldn't be able to concentrate when it's so cold. I suppose you—" She turned as she was speaking and broke off when she realised Piers was not beside her, as she had thought.

He was already at the far end of the room, standing by the open door.

"And this is my office."

This too was a large room, although smaller than the boardroom. Two walls were lined with bookshelves, painted cream and now housing only sales brochures, reference books and computer disks. The other walls were panelled to the ceiling, except at the far end, where most of the wall was taken up with a huge marble fireplace and overmantel. Two leather chesterfields stood before the hearth, and almost in the centre of the room was a large mahogany desk, littered with papers, files and a laptop computer.

"*Sarah.*"

Jez spun round. "I beg your pardon?"

"Sorry?"

"I thought you said something."

Piers shook his head. "Must have been a creaky board, or the wind."

Jez looked around the room. "So this is your office. The walls seem a bit plain."

"I know. Like I said, I have some original oil paintings for this room. They were actually painted for this house, but they are pretty dark, so I've sent them away for cleaning." The telephone shrilled and Piers walked to the desk to pick it up. There was a brief conversation then he said, "If you'll excuse me, I have to sort something out. Will you wait for me here? There's a few business magazines on the shelves over there."

"Sure. I'll be fine, don't worry."

Alone in the room, Jez sat down on one of the chesterfields. The leather was hard and cold but soon warmed to her body heat and she leaned back, revelling in the luxury. She took out her notebook to write up her notes, but her pen remained poised above the paper.

Chapter Twenty-two

The tambour frame lay untouched on Sarah's lap, as she sat before the fire, crying quietly. When the door opened, she hastily wiped her eyes and picked up her embroidery. The earl came across and stooped to drop a kiss on her brow. He hesitated, put a finger under her chin and obliged her to look up at him.

"What's this, madam, more tears?"

"I'm sorry, my lord."

He dropped to his knees before her, taking her hands in his own strong grasp.

"Sarah, Sarah. What can I do to make you smile?"

"Oh, sir, let me go back to my family."

With an angry exclamation he jumped to his feet.

"That, madam, is the one thing I cannot do! I love you too much to let you go. Besides, what is there for you at Burford that *I* cannot give you?"

She looked at him reproachfully.

"Sir, I have a husband there, and my children."

"Husband, hah! A dolt who does not love you or appreciate how far above him you are—and children—well, I can give you children."

"You can give me bastards!" she cried, throwing aside her

embroidery. She ran to him, and taking his hands in her own she looked up at him, her eyes pleading. "My lord, what we do here is a sin. Every day we live together, we descend deeper into our transgressions. Richard, Richard, you jeopardise your own soul!"

He stared down at her, his mouth twisted in a wry smile.

"But without you, Sarah, my soul is worthless. No, madam, you came here of your own free will—"

"I came here, my lord, because you threatened to ruin my husband if I did not."

"And I have kept my bargain with you. Thomas Methven is a wealthy, respected man ...and he seems to bear *your* loss with admirable fortitude—"

"What would you have done if he had come after me, if he had insisted on taking me home?"

The smile did not change, but Sarah shivered as she looked into the mocking, ice-cold eyes.

"You would be with me still, madam, but a widow. No, no, Sarah, look not so sad—it did not happen. Your family has come to no harm, so can you not love me?"

She turned from him and said in a low voice, "I am here, my lord. I will live in your house, eat at your table, wear the clothes you buy me and share your bed. Pray ask no more of me."

"But I would have you *love* me! Ah Sarah, Sarah—you live with me, eat with me and sleep with me—I have even commissioned your likeness to hang in this very room—did I not bring that damned fellow Reynolds all the way back from Devonshire just for that purpose? I would give you anything, *anything*, my dear—will you not say you love me?"

Keeping her face averted, she closed her eyes tightly,

forbidding the tears that threatened to spill over.

"We have sinned, my lord, before man and before God. There is no happiness for us. The only way to save your soul, my dear lord, is to let me go away from you and to repent your wicked ways."

"You promised to stay with me."

"And I will, sir. Until you release me from that vow, I am bound to you."

"I can't, I *won't* do it." He pulled her roughly into his arms, his fierce eyes burning into her very heart. "I will make you love me!"

She looked up at him, praying he would not realise how much she already cared for him. His anger boiled over into a red-hot rage.

"By God, madam, why do you look at me like that? Why do your eyes accuse me?"

He kissed her, gently at first, then more passionately. Sarah forced herself to stand passively in his arms until he let her go. He broke away, panting, then with an oath he spun her around and threw her down over the desk. She stifled a cry as her face hit the hard wooden surface. He was leaning over her, forcing her down.

"You say you are here for my pleasure, is that not so?" he growled, pulling up her skirts. "Well, I will show you my pleasure, madam! This way, so those great accusing eyes of yours cannot look at me!"

§

Jez had no idea how long she had been asleep, but the office had grown very dark as the spring day drew to an early close. Her notepad and pen had slipped to the floor and she bent to pick them up and put them back in her bag. The effort made her head spin and she leaned to one side, resting her forehead against the cool leather arm of the chesterfield, hoping the faintness would soon pass.

"Sarah."

It was no more than a whisper, the sigh of a breeze, but a shiver ran down her spine. She tried to move, but found her limbs would not obey her.

"I'll make you love me."

Jez was immobilised by fear. Someone was behind her: she could feel his breath on her neck, the hint of sandalwood in her nostrils.

"I'll never let you go, Sarah."

Panic overwhelmed her. Something—someone was pushing against her, pressing her down. She could not cry out, and felt herself falling, tumbling into blackness.

"Jez. Jez?"

The voice came to her from a great distance. Something icy pressed on her brow and she stirred, trying to evade the coldness. She opened her eyes to find Drina McIntosh wiping her face with a damp cloth. Over Drina's immaculately tailored shoulder Jez saw Piers looking down at her. She realised that she was stretched out on the chesterfield and began to struggle.

"Easy now." Drina helped her to sit up.

"What happened, Jez?" Piers moved round to sit on the edge of the chesterfield, taking one of her hands and chafing it gently between his own. "We found you in a dead faint. Do you know any reason for that?"

Jez stared at him blankly for a few moments, then her

hand clutched at his.

"I—I remember you leaving me..."

"Are you prone to fainting fits?" he asked.

"No, no I'm not." She looked down, checking her clothing, surprised to see that everything was still in order, her tights in place and blouse neatly buttoned, yet she felt bruised, violated.

"Who—who found me?"

It was Drina who answered.

"Piers and I were coming back this way when we heard you cry out. You gave us quite a shock, you know. How do you feel now?"

"A bit shaky." She tried to stand and Piers put a hand under her elbow to support her.

"Come on, you'd better come upstairs and I'll find you something to drink. It's all right, Drina, you can go back to the office. I'll look after her." He put an arm about Jez and led her across the room. "We'll have to use the servants' entrance."

As Drina went back to the boardroom, Piers led Jez out through the opposite door and onto a small landing. "This is the service stairs—the entrance to my apartment. Can you manage the stairs?"

"Of course. What's the alternative, you'll carry me?"

He squeezed her arm.

"Good girl."

He led her up the thickly carpeted stair to a single door, which he quickly unlocked and helped her inside. After the attention to historical detail in the main house, the apartment was surprisingly modern. It was decorated throughout in white and cream with a pale wooden floor. Everything was glass and chrome except two huge creamy leather sofas in the lounge. He gently pushed her down onto one.

"Sit down. Tea, coffee, or something stronger?"

"Tea, please."

He disappeared into the small kitchen and returned a moment later. "It won't be long. Can you remember anything?"

She shook her head.

"Not pregnant, are you?"

"No, of course not!"

"Well, it's the second time you've passed out when I've been around—you're giving me a complex about it. Perhaps you should see your doctor, just for a checkup."

"Yes, I might do that." She felt close to tears. "I'm sorry. I've spoiled your day."

"Not at all." He sat down opposite her and watched her closely.

"Do you live here?" she asked, disliking the silence.

"Only when I need to stay in town. I have a house in the country, near Bath."

"Oh, yes. Of course."

"What do you mean, of course?"

Jez frowned. "I don't know, I just thought—have you told me that before?"

"No, I don't think so." Piers went off to fetch her tea.

"It must be like living over the shop, staying here. Can you ever get away from your work?"

"Yes, when I want to. I can disable the lift, switch the phone back to reception and ignore everyone. Here, try that."

He handed her a cup.

"Thanks."

She sipped it gratefully. Earl Grey. No one else ever gave her Earl Grey unless she asked for it by name.

"How do you feel now?"

"Much better, thank you."

"Good. How did you get here, by the way, on the train? I'll have someone drive you home. I'd do it myself but I've a meeting..."

"No! No, that's not necessary. I'm fine now. Please—please don't make a fuss."

"Are you sure?"

"Yes. I just want to—" *To get out of this house* were the words she could not say. "To get back to Luxbury. I'm really fine now, promise."

"I'll get someone to take you back to the station and see you on the train home."

"That's very good of you." She picked up her bag and prepared to follow him out of the room. "Piers?"

"Hmm?"

"You didn't...touch me? When I was unconscious, I mean?"

"No, of course not. I came in with Drina. Why?"

"I don't know. I just thought—" She shivered.

Piers took her by the shoulders and stared at her.

"What's wrong, Jez? What are you trying to say? Are you frightened of me?"

She met his eyes quite candidly. "I've never been afraid of you."

His sudden, warm smile comforted her.

"Good. Come on, then. Let's find Drina. I'll phone you."

"Please don't."

But she knew he would.

When she looked in the mirror the next morning, Jez saw a

black bruise forming on her cheekbone.

Chapter Twenty-three

Jez sat before the little gas fire in her great aunt's living room, holding her mug tightly between her hands. It was Friday night: she had arrived at her aunt's house only twenty minutes earlier and had allowed herself to be fussed over and petted, sitting obediently while Emmy made tea and set a plate of tempting fruitcake slices before her.

"You look worn out, love," said Emmy. "And that mark on your cheek looks pretty nasty. What's happened?"

Jez was thankful for the prompt. She had decided she would tell Emmy everything she could, but still her cheeks burned with embarrassment.

"I—um—I don't know, Emmy. I'm either being haunted or I'm going mad."

Emmy smiled. "Well, I don't believe in ghosts, but I'm certain you're not crazy. Tell me it all."

Jez drew a breath and began, slowly at first, but determined not to miss anything. She started with the dreams, half-remembered images and emotions that disturbed her. She told her aunt about Piers, too, and the strange occurrences at the Manor.

Emmy listened silently as Jez poured out everything that had happened to her over the past few months: her dislike of being alone in the dining room of Lilac Cottage, the unexplained fainting fits at the Manor and Cordeaux House—even repeating the story of old Tom protecting Sarah's grave.

"I—I don't know what to do, Aunt Emmy. I'm—scared now to be alone."

Emmy set down her mug.

"This—Piers, the young man who owns CME. You said that when you were snowbound at the hotel it was the *second* time you had stayed there with him?"

"Yes."

The old lady's sharp eyes watched her carefully.

"So what happened the first time, Jessica?"

"Nothing—nothing odd."

"I'm not talking about the supernatural, child, I mean you and Piers. Did you sleep with him?" Jez bit her lip. Emmy smiled. "Just because I'm old and single doesn't mean I don't know what goes on in the world, my love. Come on, you can tell me. I'm quite broad-minded."

"Well—yes."

"And since then?"

"Nothing. I told him about Harry."

"But you still find him attractive."

Jez sighed. "Oh yes!"

"Well my dear, I'm no psychiatrist but it seems pretty clear to me. Think about it. On two occasions when you have been in the company of this man you have fainted and dreamed that some—some *thing* has tried to seduce you. Wouldn't it be a far more reasonable explanation that you have been suppressing your feelings for this man to such an extent that your subconscious has taken over?"

"That's what Piers said."

"You've told him all this?"

"Uh huh."

"You seem to be on very good terms with someone who's harassing you."

Jez flushed.

"He doesn't harass me. And—well, I can talk to him, Emmy. I don't know why, I just feel comfortable in his company." Emmy closed her lips on the observation she was about to make and presently Jez spoke again. "In any case, that doesn't explain everything. What about the chill in the dining room?"

"Sheer imagination."

"And old Tom's story?"

"Now that, I admit, is more interesting. There could be a grain of truth in it, though. Perhaps the story has been handed down through his family, embellished and elaborated with each telling. The part about this ghostly duke could have been added at any time."

"You really think so?"

"Yes, my dear child, I do. I'm afraid we've been filling your head with all this silly nonsense and there you are, stuck all alone in that little cottage—it's hardly surprising your mind starts playing tricks on you."

"There is one last thing, Emmy. Piers says that a couple of times I've called out the name Richard in my sleep. The mysterious *R*. It could be the name of Sarah's lover."

"It could. Or it might just be a name you've taken a fancy to." Emmy rose. "What you need is a couple of good nights' sleep, so let's get your bed made up and you can get an early night. From the look of you, it won't be too soon!"

When Jessica awoke the sun was streaming through the

window of the little bedroom. She stretched luxuriously and picked up her watch. Ten o'clock. Reaching for her dressing gown, she slipped out of bed and went in search of her aunt. She found her in the kitchen.

"So, you're awake at last. Would you like breakfast? Bacon and eggs?"

"Mm, yes, please."

"How did you sleep?"

"Like a log. I can't remember anything. Perhaps you're right, Emmy, I've been overdoing it. All I needed was a break."

"Let's hope so. Now go and get yourself dressed while I'm cooking, and after that we'll stroll down to the village hall. It's the Spring Craft Fair this afternoon."

"When's Harry due back?"

Jez and Aunt Emmy were walking across the ancient village green towards the small community centre. Even from this distance Jez could see the garish banner stretched above the door.

"He rang yesterday to say he's coming home in a fortnight." Jez turned her face up to the sun. She'd been so busy working indoors, at CME, in the cottage and the restaurant, she'd forgotten how good fresh air could be.

"Have you told him? About the dreams, I mean, and the fainting—"

"No." Jez dug her hands into her pockets. "It's never seemed like the right moment. Besides, I don't want to worry him while he's so far away. It's not as if he can do anything."

"True. But you should tell him."

"You never know, it might all be over by the time he gets back. Then there'll be no need." She grinned. "Perhaps it's all

203

over now, exorcised by your common-sense explanation, Emmy!"

They stepped into the hall and into another world. There was a buzz of chattering voices as the crowd milled about the room. Colourful stalls had been set up selling local pottery, handwoven baskets and embroidered napkins alongside the obligatory cakes, tombola and the white elephant stall. Squeezed between one table full of bright purple pots and another displaying shell-covered boxes was a herb stall.

Jez stopped. Amongst the packets of sage and thyme were lesser-known herbs like fenugreek, wormwood and valerian.

The woman behind the table was dressed as a gypsy, a brightly coloured shawl over her shoulders and large hooped earrings dangling beneath her black curls. Her dark eyes stared at Jessica. "Are you interested in herbs, dearie?"

"No-o, I don't know that much about them."

"They're steeped in history and folklore, you know, and there's something for every occasion—valerian to help you sleep, tarragon root for toothache, herb-willow for sore eyes, but for you, my dear, I'd suggest borage to drive away your sorrow."

Jez grinned, shaking her head.

"No, thank you. I'm fine. I don't need anything."

"Don't you? Come, lass, you can tell me what's haunting you."

"Why do you say that?" Jez countered, a little sharply, and the woman gave a sly smile.

"You've the look about you. Give me your hand." She reached out and caught Jez's fingers. "Yes, I can feel it. You're troubled by spirits."

Jez laughed uncertainly. "I don't believe in ghosts and all

that sort of thing—pure superstition."

"Is it?" The woman stared at her with no trace of amusement in her face. "Trust your feelings, young lady. There are no clear-cut answers for you, no ghostly rattling of chains and figures disappearing through the wall. A spirit is more like a moon shadow, pale and very often indiscernible to us in our modern world of bright lights and fast living. It's a special gift, to be aware of the spirits."

A cold tingle ran the length of Jez's spine. She wanted to challenge this, to ask the woman what she knew, but people were pushing past her to buy the herbs, holding up the packets and coins, and the gypsy woman turned away to attend to her customers. The moment was gone.

Jez looked around for Emmy, who was crossing the hall with her arms full of mismatched pottery and a very yellow dried flower arrangement.

"There you are, Jez, have you had enough? Shall we go? Perhaps you could give me a hand to carry some of this. Oh dear, I know what you're thinking, and you are right, I should never have bought it. I don't even like the pottery much, but it's all in a good cause, isn't it? And I can see the trip has done you good, it's put some colour in your cheeks at last."

Another good night's sleep seemed to confirm Emmy's optimism. Jez hummed a tune as she helped her aunt prepare the lunch.

"By the way, Emmy, how was your trip to London? You were just about to climb into the taxi when I phoned, remember?"

"Mm. It was very nice, dear. I went to spend a few days with an old friend."

"Oho! A secret admirer."

"No-o, nothing like that."

"Well? What is it then?"

"If all this family history is affecting you, Jez, I don't know if I should tell you."

"Tell me what, for goodness' sake?"

Emmy's face glowed with excitement.

"It's the letter. You know, the charred one we found in Sarah's box. My friend in London used to work at the Preservation Unit in St. Pancras—where they restore old books and manuscripts, etc. Well, I took the letter with me and asked him if he could do anything. You remember how badly burned it was, we were afraid to touch it. Well, he took it to his friends at the Unit and asked them to look at it, and they managed to open it. It is very fragile of course, so they have kept the original, but I have a copy."

"No! That's wonderful news, Auntie. Can I see it? Oh Emmy, don't look like that—you *can't* mean to tell me all this and *not* let me look at it. I promise you I won't let it upset me."

After a brief hesitation, Emmy fetched the copy of Sarah's letter. Jez took it, aware that her hand was trembling. The thin copy paper was nothing like the crackling parchment of the original, but she recognised the fine, sloping characters that covered the page.

"It's Sarah's."

"Yes."

"'My dear J'—can that be Jenny, her daughter?" She looked at her aunt, who nodded.

"Look at the date, dear. 1762. Jenny would have been about nineteen."

"'Darling child, if this letter—' Then there's a gap where the paper is burnt away. 'I pray you will n—' It's burnt away there, too. '—without perusing its contents. It is from one who loves you and who wants nothing more than your hap—' I guess that the word there is happiness! '...have been told that your mother is no longer... That is untrue and you are of an age now when you deserve the truth. Your father has kept from you the reasons I left but believe me it was a decision forced upon me to protect you and your brother from total ruin, nothing else would have taken me from my place at your father's side. I...news of my family from one of the servants, but I must mention no names for fear of retribution on that... I learned you are about to marry. My dear, I am so happy for you. I understand that he is a good and honest man, sincerely attached to you. I will pray for your happiness—you have been deprived of a mother's love and advice all these years, dear Jennifer, but now I believe I must make a push to contact you, to tell you to learn from my mistakes...and would not have you suffer as I have done. I have sinned and the penance has been severe. I have no expectation of your forgiveness, my dear child, although perhaps in time you may understand why I was forced to take this path. Now my only hope...God's forgiveness...I will endeavour to have this letter delivered to you secretly. There are those in...still think kindly of me, although they dare not defend me openly before him. Believe me that these words come with the prayers of one who loves you deeply and who will always be...your mother, Sarah Methven.'"

When she had finished, Jez read the letter again while her aunt watched her in silence.

"If I remember," Jez said at last, "the seal on this letter was unbroken. No-one had read it."

"Exactly. Somehow it arrived in the Methven household, probably fell into Thomas' hands and he threw it into the fire immediately."

"And one of the servants—one of those Sarah said still

thought kindly of her—rescued it but dared not give it to Jenny."

"Very likely the housekeeper or someone who had known Sarah well, because they risked being dismissed if Thomas found they were keeping Sarah's letters against his wishes. It's a miracle that it's survived. Imagine: it's been lying there all these years, unread."

Until now, thought Jez. Maybe she's trying to tell us, to tell *me* something.

Chapter Twenty-four

After reading Sarah Methven's letter to her daughter, Jez felt confident she knew now where she was going. Her studies would be over in a few months, then she and Harry could really begin a new life together. She could get a job abroad, if he wanted to continue working in Germany—the important thing was that they would be together. She told Harry as much when he telephoned and was touched by his concern that she shouldn't neglect her own career.

"You don't speak the language, Jez," he had said. "You would be far better placed to get a good position in London, or even the States. You've got to think of your future."

"I know, Harry, but we've hardly seen each other for the past few months—I want to give some time to us."

She had had to be content with Harry's assurance that there would be plenty of time to discuss everything when he came home, but she felt confident now that she knew what she wanted. Piers Cordeaux was no longer in the picture.

Jez spotted the silver Aston Martin in the car park as soon as she arrived at CME on Thursday morning. Despite her insistence that she didn't care about Piers Cordeaux, the thought of seeing him again was not unpleasant, and she found her eyes flicking to the office door every time it opened. When

Piers did eventually enter the office, he headed straight for her desk. Lavinia had disappeared to the other end of the building and Jez was alone in that area—a mixed blessing, she thought as she watched Piers moving towards her. His smile made her catch her breath. The tug of attraction was as strong as ever.

"Hi. How are you? Did you get home safely on the train last week?"

"Of course." She thought her voice was a little breathless, and hoped he would not notice. "I'm sorry I was such a nuisance."

"Drina sends her best wishes to you."

"Oh—that's very kind of her."

"Jez—"

She felt the panic rising.

"Please, Piers. You'll have to excuse me, I'm very busy today." She turned to her PC and attacked the keyboard furiously.

He did not walk away, but perched on the edge of her desk. She did not look at him but she could almost feel his eyes on her. She bit her lip and continued typing.

"Do you mind if I sit here and watch you?"

"No. Stay there by all means, if you've nothing better to do."

"I won't put you off?"

"Not at all." She stared hard at her handwritten notes, her fingers continuing to fly over the keys.

"Then why are you typing rubbish into your computer?"

She paused and looked at the screen. The jumble of letters made no sense at all. She felt her face go red.

Piers laughed softly. "So you don't care about me, huh?"

"Oh go away!" she hissed.

She noticed with relief that Lavinia was coming back to her desk. With a lazy grin Piers stood up and turned to greet his marketing manager.

"Hi, Vinnie. I was just saying to Jez that I haven't seen you since the seminar. Are you and Jimmy Hartley-Paige still seeing each other?"

Lavinia's usually cool cheeks were tinged with pink.

"Well, yes, actually. In fact, we're going to Derbyshire for the weekend." She looked up at Piers, smiling. "I was really very grateful for the chance to stay in Birmingham on the night of the seminar, Piers. I never did get round to thanking you for bringing Jez home, and with the weather so bad, too. Jez told me you'd had to put up at the Manor."

Jez held her breath. What would he say? She had played down the incident when Vinnie had quizzed her about her journey home, but it only needed one look, the slightest hint of embarrassment, and tongues would start to wag. To her relief Piers merely shrugged.

"Since it's part of my chain they could hardly turn us away. It was a nuisance, but that's all. And anyway, I was glad to help you, Vinnie. Always pleased to assist the course of true love. Perhaps you can do the same for me some time."

Lavinia laughed as Piers strolled off. "Well, he's cheerful today. Something must be going right for him."

Jez did not comment. She was only thankful that Vinnie's own love life was going so well she was oblivious to anything else.

Jez did not see Piers again, and she drove away from the office not knowing if she was pleased or sorry that he had kept away from her. She had travelled some miles when she realised that she was being followed. The silver Aston Martin filled her rear-view mirror, and she stared at it for so long that she nearly ran off the road. At first she thought that he would turn off at the roundabout and head for the motorway, but he remained behind her. She drove on, glancing frequently into the mirror, her temper rising steadily. When they reached the long straight leading into Luxbury, she angrily ground down through the gears and pulled into a lay-by. The Aston Martin cruised to a halt behind her. Muttering under her breath, Jez jumped out of her car.

"What the hell do you think you are doing?"

Piers looked unperturbed at her outburst. "Following you home."

She almost ground her teeth in frustration.

"I don't need an escort, thank you very much."

"Oh don't worry, I won't bother you."

"But you *are* bothering me! Go away."

"All right—on one condition."

She looked at him suspiciously.

"Look me in the eyes and tell me you never want to see me again." He waited. "Well?" She stared down at his handsome face. Her hand positively itched to slap it, especially when he grinned and said again, "Well, Jez?"

"Oh—do what you want!" She turned on her heel but he caught her wrist.

"I want—I *want* to be with you, Jessica Skelton. I wanted to tell you how much I liked having you in my house."

"What's that supposed to mean?"

"In London—when I was showing you round. It felt—I don't know—right, somehow, that you should be there."

"That's ridiculous."

"Maybe. All I know is that I can't get you out of my mind." The laughter had gone from his voice now. "I see you walking through the boardroom, sitting in my office, in my rooms—the house has never felt so lonely before."

He was serious. Jez felt her heart thudding painfully in her chest. She could not trust herself to speak. Gently she pulled her hand from his grasp and began to walk away.

"I'll ring you," he called after her.

She stopped. "No, don't."

She walked back to her car. As she pulled away she glanced in her mirror. The Aston Martin remained in the lay-by.

Jez drove home with her mind in turmoil. How dare he follow her! It had been bad enough that he had disrupted her work, upsetting her concentration for the rest of the day, but to have the audacity to follow her—who did he think he was? The sudden blaring of a car horn brought her back to reality and she swerved back into her own lane, slowing down and trying to ignore the angry gesturing of the driver in the car beside her. She concentrated on getting to Luxbury in one piece.

When she reached the High Street Jez parked the car and sat for a few moments, fuming inwardly. Why was she allowing him to have this effect on her? She took a few deep, calming breaths. She would take a nice relaxing bath, maybe light a few scented candles—she might even ring Kate for a chat. The thought of such indulgence restored her to some semblance of good humour and she was even humming a tune as she unlocked the cottage door, but the music died on her lips as she stepped inside.

Two bulging suitcases stood in the lounge. She was still staring at them when Harry walked out of the kitchen.

"Hello, Jez."

"H-Harry! What—what a nice surprise." Her voice sounded hollow even to her own ears but Harry did not appear to notice.

"I managed to get away a week early. Sorry I couldn't tell you—I didn't know myself 'til the last minute and had to rush to get the connection..."

She felt she was stumbling around in a dream. Her brain refused to work.

"No problem. Have—have you eaten? I haven't much in—"

"No, no—look, I know this sounds crazy, but I've got to go out again. Something's come up. But when I get back, we'll talk."

"Yes—all right."

"Mm, well, okay then. I'll just get these cases upstairs..."

Jez wandered through to the kitchen. Harry was home. She had wished for it for so long, but now he was here and she felt—nothing. He had not kissed her. In fact, there was a definite awkwardness between them. A chill ran through her. Perhaps he knew about Piers. She made coffee, trying to sort out the jumble of thoughts and emotions that crowded her brain. She heard his footsteps coming downstairs.

"Harry? Harry, I want to tell you—"

"Yeah, yeah Jez, I know. We have to talk, but let's leave it 'til I get back, all right? I won't be long. Couple of hours, promise."

"But you've only just got in—"

He flushed, looking more than ever like a guilty schoolboy.

"I know, but it's a call I've got to make. I'd have stopped on the way from the airport if I'd flown into East Midlands, but I could only get a flight to Heathrow." He kissed her cheek. "See you later."

He was gone. Jez thought ruefully of her plans for his homecoming: the fire in the dining room, candlelit dinner. It had all gone so wrong. Suddenly the telephone's urgent call split the silence.

"Jez? If I apologise for this afternoon, will you meet me for dinner?"

"No, Piers, I've got work to do."

"Then I'll come round there..."

"No!"

"I have to see you Jez."

"No. You can't." She paused. "Harry's home."

"Oh. Is he there now?"

"No, no. He's back from Germany but he's had to go out for a while."

"Then come and meet me for a drink. I want to talk to you." She did not answer and he continued, "You know the Old Sun, the pub on the North Road out of Luxbury? I'll see you there."

"Piers, I can't."

"Jez, you *can*. I'll see you there in half an hour. If you don't turn up I shall come and get you."

The thought of Piers hammering on her door and the subsequent gossip persuaded her. She ran upstairs to change her glasses for contact lenses—nothing to do with seeing Piers, she told herself—she preferred her lenses in the evening. A quick comb through her hair, then she picked up her bag and car keys and left the house.

Piers was waiting for her in the lounge of the Old Sun. He had replaced his suit jacket with a navy sweater, but she spotted him immediately. He was taller than anyone else at the bar, and it occurred to her that he had an aura of success about him, something indefinable that attracted the eye—at

215

least it attracted *her* eyes as she entered the pub. It was a popular meeting place on the edge of Luxbury, its oak beams and stone fireplace decorated with an overabundance of brass. Service at the bar was swift and efficient, although Jez detected a look of disdain in the barman's eyes as he poured her mineral water and set it down beside Piers' fruit juice—there would be little profit to be made from their custom this evening. They took their drinks to a small table in the corner.

She searched her mind for something to say. "I saw you on TV a while ago. On the news."

"Oh yes. The American deal."

"Is it going through?"

"Maybe. There's a lot to discuss yet."

She looked at him over her glass.

"Why are you here, Piers?"

"I just wanted to see you."

"Well, I'm here."

"Yes. Thanks for coming." She shrugged, saying nothing. "How's Harry getting on in his job?"

"Harry? Oh, he loves it."

"And he's back a week early."

"How do you know about that?"

"When I told you I'd heard of Tarrant International, it wasn't quite the truth. Actually, I have a seat on the board."

"So?"

"So I've been taking an...interest in Harry's career."

She stared at him. "Are you saying you—you *arranged* for him to get his place on the Cologne project?"

"Let's say I may have influenced the decision."

"But Harry's a good engineer!"

216

"Undoubtedly. They wouldn't keep him if he wasn't."

"Just what are you trying to say to me, Piers?"

He stared at his glass, turning it round and round on the table. "What would Harry think if he knew he owed his promotion to his girlfriend's...connections?"

"Are you trying to blackmail me?"

"That's an unpleasant term."

"It's an unpleasant thought. What do you want, Piers?"

"You."

"And you think this is the way to get me?"

He shrugged. "I've tried everything else. I'm getting desperate."

A cold chill spread through her as she thought of Sarah Methven, alone, unhappy, unfaithful. Strange, old-world words came unbidden to her tongue.

"You think to force my compliance with your demands?"

Piers frowned at her.

"That's an antiquated way of putting it. But—no. I'm not saying I wouldn't have tried it, if I thought there was a chance of success, but it wouldn't work, would it? That would only make you hate me. No. I just wanted you to know about my connection with Tarrant. I wanted to be honest with you."

"Thanks." She knew she sounded bitter, but she felt too numb, too tired to try any more.

"What is it Jez? Why won't you admit the attraction between us?"

She felt her throat tighten as tears threatened, making it difficult to speak.

"It's—well..." Her hand waved vaguely. "You have—everything."

217

He laughed at that, mocking and without humour.

"Oh, my God! That great British tradition of sticking with the underdog. Look, Jez—I admit I'm successful, but Harry's only, what—twenty-five, twenty-six? You said yourself he's good, and he's ambitious. Who knows where he'll be in ten years' time? And what will you do then, find someone else to pity?"

"No! It's isn't like that."

"Then what *is it* like?"

She sought desperately for words to explain. "Harry trusts me."

"Then be honest with him!" He leaned closer, lowering his voice. "Give the three of us a break, Jez."

She coloured angrily. "What would you have me say to him? That I've been sleeping around while he's been working his bollocks off in Cologne?"

"But you don't love him any more, do you? Do you?"

"I—I don't know."

"I'm not asking you to swear undying love to me, Jez. I just want to give this thing between us a chance." He put down his glass. "I won't wait any longer, Jez."

She shook her head, trying to get her thoughts into some coherent order. She was torn between Harry, dear, dependable Harry, on the first rung of his chosen career, and the man who had everything—cars, houses, a successful business—how could she choose Piers without everyone thinking she was a gold-digger?

Piers seemed to read her mind. He shrugged.

"Final chance, Jez. Time to choose. Look. This is *me*. This is what I am. If I lost everything tomorrow I would still be the same person, can't you see that? But I can't prove it to you by throwing it all away. I too have commitments—you remember you said I wasn't familiar with that term? Well, there are hundreds, probably thousands of people depending on me for a livelihood. My success is also theirs. I can't turn my back on everything I've worked for, even for you. I'm sorry Jez. I've tried everything to reach you. You know we belong together—it's in your eyes, in the way you respond to me when I touch you, but you won't admit it. I don't want to cheat, or lie. I want us to have a straightforward, honest relationship. Who knows, it might burn itself out in a year, or even a few months. I don't know. But I *do* know that I love you. I've never felt like this about anyone before, and I believe you feel the same way about me. If only you'd stop being so damned noble!" He pulled his mobile phone from his pocket. "Has Harry got a mobile? Okay, then ring him, Jez. Ring Harry right now and tell him it's over."

She stared at the phone, her body tense. Her own words ran through her head. *A promise is a promise, Emmy. You can't just make a commitment then walk away from it.* Sarah had done that, and look what had happened to her.

"No. I can't."

Piers did not move. He looked at her for a long moment, then he sighed. He said gently, "Okay, okay, I won't torment you—or me, for that matter—any more. We could have been so good together, but—if that's what you want... Goodbye, Jez."

Chapter Twenty-five

"It's over."

The words rattled around in her brain as she drove back to Lilac Cottage. She felt strangely calm, driving automatically, her emotions suspended. The glare of headlights from the oncoming traffic was almost hypnotic, and she could hear the words *gone, gone,* in the whoosh of passing cars.

"Well you've done it, girl," she said aloud. "He won't be bothering you anymore."

She had chosen. She should be happy—Piers was out of her life, she was free to concentrate on working things out with Harry. Somehow the thought made her want to cry, but she felt too drained even for tears, and her eyes felt gritty and dry. Good thing, too, she told herself bitterly. If you cry now, you'll probably lose a lens. She parked her car and walked slowly to the cottage. In all the mess of emotions churning within her was one certainty: she did not love Harry. It came as a revelation, but not a surprise. Jez thought that perhaps she had known for a long time—the irony was that she had had to lose Piers to discover her true feelings.

Her steps dragged as she entered the cottage. Harry was standing in the lounge, his hands dug deep into his pockets. She struggled to smile. Why had it become such hard work to think? Her eyes wandered to the suitcases at the foot of the stairs. Surely he had taken them upstairs when he came in earlier. Upstairs—suddenly the thought of sharing a bed with him was not to be borne. They both started to speak.

"Harry, I'm sorry, but—"

"Jez, let me say my bit first—I've been going over it in my mind all the way back here, and if you stop me now I'll never get it out. Why don't you sit down?"

She sank onto the sofa. Harry paced before her, his boyish face frowning, serious. At last he stopped pacing and ran a hand through his fair hair.

"Look, Jez, there's no easy way to say this. You know things have been—strained between us while I've been in Cologne. Well, it's because there's someone else—"

So he knew. Her face flushed.

"How did you—"

"How did I meet her? She was at Tarrant when I started, and we've been working together in Germany. Charlie's on the project team, like me. I think I've mentioned her to you. It—it started before Christmas, really. When you're working closely with someone sometimes it—it just happens." He looked at her, misreading her look of astonishment. "Jez, I'm sorry! Maybe I should have told you sooner, but—I wanted to tell you face to face, not over the phone. And—well, I thought perhaps that once I got back, that perhaps we could make a fresh start, but—Charlie flew back last week, you see, and she phoned me just before I left, so I promised to go and see her—"

"I—I—"

"Oh God, I'm so sorry, Jessica!"

"What—what will you do?"

"Um—I'm going to stay with Charlie. Look, I don't like to leave you like this. Do you want me to make you a coffee before

221

I go?"

She stared into his anxious eyes and fought down an insane desire to laugh. She tried to concentrate on her breathing, to focus on the situation.

"No, thanks. I'll be all right."

"You're sure? I can ring Charlie and explain—"

"No, there's no need for that. You'd better go, Harry."

"Yes." He picked up the cases. "Well. Goodbye then."

"Harry?" She stood up and turned to look at him.

"Yes?"

"Leave me the door key."

"Oh, yes. Of course." He handed over the key and after a brief hesitation he leaned forwards and kissed her cheek.

"Goodbye, Jez."

She remained standing for some moments after he had gone, the quiet of the house gathering around her. The silence was comforting. She sighed.

"And then there were none."

§

"Sarah."

"My lord." Roused from her reverie, Sarah turned from the window and smiled at the earl.

He was dressed for riding in a plain dark coat, buckskins and top boots, and as he crossed the room he dropped his hat and gloves onto a chair. He kissed her lightly then held her away from him, his eyes searching her face. She knew there would be signs of tears but he did not mention it.

"Tell me what you have done today."

"Today, sir? I—a little embroidery, the final sitting for my portrait—I do hope you will approve it, my lord. Mr. Reynolds assures me it will be one of his best."

"And have you received any letters, Sarah?"

"Letters, sir? I—"

"I know you will not lie to me, sweeting, so I will make it easier for you. I know that you have today received a letter from your husband."

"Oh."

He led her to the sofa and obliged her to sit beside him.

"May I see it?"

She hung her head. "I have burned it."

"I can guess its contents."

Sarah sighed.

"I had written to Thomas, asking—asking that I might be allowed to see the children. He has forbidden it. He says the children have been told that I...that I am dead."

"The devil he has! Damn him, I'll make him tell them the truth."

She clutched his arm.

"No! No, sir, I pray you will not. I know you are powerful, that you could force him to do your will, but it would only make him hate me more and cause the children further suffering. Thomas is a good man, my lord, and he has been most grievously wronged."

"If he was a Christian he would forgive you—"

She smiled a little at that.

"Nay, he would needs be a saint, after what I have done to

him. But I do miss my children so!"

With a groan he fell on his knees before her, catching her hands in his own.

"Oh Sarah, Sarah, why do you persist in defending your husband? He has made it abundantly clear he wants nothing more to do with you, while I—I worship you, my dear. I want only to make you happy."

She smiled down at him, pulling one hand free to caress his lean cheek.

"Yet it is *you* who caused my ruin," she said quietly.

He buried his face in her skirts.

"I know it, yet I could not help myself. Oh Sarah, forgive me!"

She stroked his dark head, blinking back her tears. "I have already done so, my lord."

"But—you cannot—love me."

She was silent. At last the earl rose to his feet and walked to the window, his hands clasped together behind his back.

"Since the day I—forced myself upon you—here, in this very room—you will acknowledge that I have not attempted to touch you again."

Sarah felt the colour rushing to her cheeks.

"You have been most forbearing, sir." Her voice was scarcely above a whisper.

"I was a brute!" he said savagely. "I have never before—I cannot forgive myself for hurting you." He sighed and said, without looking round. "If I cannot make you happy, then there is only one thing to be done."

"My lord?"

He turned to face her.

"You are convinced that we are damned for breaking our marriage vows. Is it too late to be saved?"

"Not if you truly repent your sins, sir."

"If that means saying I regret loving you, Sarah, I cannot do it."

"Oh, my dear lord. I would not have you damned for my sake."

"Too late, my love! But—you are convinced we can never be happy."

"There can be no happiness in sin, Richard."

He turned from her to stare again out the window. Sarah looked at him, loving every line, every detail of his tall, graceful frame.

"Very well. I will release you."

She stared at him, the colour draining from her cheeks.

"What—what did you say?"

"I will let you go." He turned. "You agreed you would not leave me until I released you from your vows. You are free to go."

She stared at him, then jumped up and ran towards him, holding out her hands.

"Oh—I—th-thank you. I—I must write again to Thomas—or perhaps my father—"

He caught her hands, saying gently, "Sarah, Sarah, be careful. You know what I have done to you. I have ruined your reputation—even when you are no longer living under my protection they may not take you back. Allow me to give you the use of a cottage on my Leicestershire estate, with a small pension until you are assured of your family's protection."

"You—you think they will not forgive me. But when I have explained—"

"It is a harsh world, Sarah. I know more of its cruelties than you, my dear, and I am very much afraid that you will be rebuffed. I may be wrong—pray God that I am. But you must promise me you will let me provide for you, if they refuse to aid you. I have ruined you, my child. God surely will not punish you for accepting this from me. Heaven knows it is small recompense for what I have taken from you. Promise me!"

She looked at him, confused.

"Y-yes, I promise, but I am sure it will not be necessary."

He let her go and walked away, saying over his shoulder, "My servant shall act as your messenger. I give you my word, love, that I shall never cross your threshold, unless you invite me to do so."

"You—you are very good, sir."

He gave a harsh laugh: "Good! No. If I was *good*, I should have left you with that doltish husband of yours. Come now, don't cry or I shall never be able to leave you. I am going to my club. I have left instructions that my carriage is to take you to Leicestershire as soon as you have packed. Martha will accompany you. She has grown attached to you and is happy enough to remain in your service for as long as you require her."

"Richard—"

"No—don't speak. I must go. You had best be gone before I return, or my resolution may desert me and I will forbid you to leave me!"

He collected his hat and gloves and walked to the door.

"God be with you, madam."

With a final bow he strode out of the room.

Chapter Twenty-six

"Well my girl, you've really cocked it up, haven't you?" Kate's eyes were not unsympathetic. When she had heard that Jez was alone she had insisted on coming round, bringing with her a take-away and a bottle of wine and demanding to know every gory little detail. "So when did all this happen?" she asked, tipping the contents of the foil containers onto two plates.

Jez uncorked the wine and carried it through to the dining room. "Last week."

"And you didn't call me?"

"I didn't want to talk to anyone."

"No, you knew we'd all say you've been a complete idiot. God, it's gloomy in here! We should have lit the fire. Never mind, if we light those candles it will cheer the place up. That's much better." She sat across the table from Jez and dug her fork into the food piled on her plate. "Yummy, I love Chinese. So why didn't you ring Piers and tell him you'd split with Harry?"

"I couldn't."

"Don't see why not. He's nuts about you—even I could see that, and I only met the guy once."

Jez slowly pushed the sweet-and-sour pork around her plate. "He just wanted what he couldn't have."

"You sure about that?"

"Yes—no—oh, I don't know any more!"

"Well, you know I always thought you were crazy to stick with Harry."

"So you told me, many times."

"He wasn't right for you, Jez."

"Obviously."

"No, I mean he wasn't the faithful caring friend you always thought him. Do you mind if I have the rest of the fried rice? Thanks. No. You were always so loyal to him and I didn't want to say anything but—well, he tried it on with me. Several times."

Jez stared at her friend.

"It's true." Kate nodded. "He rang me a few times to ask me out—the last time was when you were away at that exhibition in October. Wanted me to have dinner with him. And whenever I came round, if you were out of the room he just couldn't keep his hands to himself."

"Oh Kate, I'm sorry!"

"Hey, why should you be sorry? It's not your fault. But that's why I didn't like to visit you when Harry was here. Just thought you ought to know. Might make you feel better about splitting up."

"Mm. Thanks."

"So what are you going to do now?"

Jez poured more wine into their glasses. "Finish my MSc, then I might take a holiday. Mum and Bruno are going to South America for a few months and they've invited me along."

It was Kate's turn to stare. "You told me you couldn't stand Bruno."

Jez shifted uncomfortably. "Perhaps I was being a bit harsh. After all, I don't really know him. I was just blaming him for coming between Mum and Dad." She managed a grin. "Anyway, it means I'll make use of my passport this year."

For the next few weeks Jez concentrated on her work. Summer was always a quiet time at the Spinning Wheel Restaurant and Malcolm reluctantly had to let her go. Jez was not too unhappy—the extra time was useful to her as she put the finishing touches to her report, a copy of which she handed in to Lavinia for company assessment. She did not see Piers. She heard from Lavinia that he was spending more time in the States. A casual enquiry elicited the information that he was not expected to visit the Filchester office for some time, certainly not before her secondment came to an end.

Despite this news, Jez found herself hoping that he might call in, and she was aware of a searing disappointment when he did not appear.

§

"So, Jez. Your last day with us." Vinnie had gathered everyone around and Jez felt her cheeks grow pink with embarrassment at such attention. "We just wanted to say how much we've enjoyed working with you, and I'd like to add a personal thank you for all the help you've given me."

Vinnie nodded at Melanie, who stepped forward, grinning broadly. She held out a brightly wrapped package.

"We had a collection for you—hope you like it."

Jez tore off the paper and held up the soft leather shoulder bag.

Melinda Hammond

"We knew you already had a nice briefcase, so we thought you could use this at weekends and things," explained Melanie, watching Jez anxiously. "It's got loads of room in it."

"It's just what I need, thank you." Jez hugged them all in turn, leaving Lavinia until the last.

"Very best of luck, Jessica—and keep in touch. I know everyone says that, but I really mean it. And if you need a job for a while just let me know. I'd have you on my marketing team any day."

Two weeks later, Jez attended her final session with her course tutor and realised that a whole chapter of her life had come to an end. She spent a few days with Emilia Appleton, putting on a brave face when her aunt asked the inevitable questions about Piers and Harry.

"Honestly, Emmy, I'm glad to be away from all men for a while. I need some space. Time to think what I'm going to do with my life."

"Are you going to stay on at the cottage?"

"Yes. At least, I will for a while, until I get my results from the university. It depends on where I get work. I'm going to put my name with a few agencies and start looking in earnest when I get back from South America."

"Oh yes—your holiday with your mother."

"Mm. I thought it was time I really got to know Bruno. I've realised that you can't spend your life resenting someone. And it's not really his fault that he and Mum fell in love, is it?"

Emmy smiled. "No, darling. I'm glad you're going to give him a chance. When do you go?"

"Three weeks' time. Beginning of July. I'll fly out to Spain and spend a week there with them first. Mother says Bruno will arrange everything from there."

"An all-expenses-paid trip, how wonderful! And away from this dreary wet summer."

"Yes." Suddenly she didn't want to think about leaving the country. "How are you getting on with your family history? Any more on Sarah Methven?"

"No. A complete blank. I suppose she was considered a disgrace to the family and they couldn't forgive her. Thank goodness we live in a more enlightened age. And you, Jessica. Not troubled by ghosts any more, are you?"

"No. All that stopped once Piers was out of my life. So it probably was what you said, all part of some emotional imbalance. Anyway, that part of my life is over, and I'm looking forward to the next part. The world is my oyster now."

Jez thought about that as she sat in the dining room of the cottage with application forms, several daily newspapers, and pages of notes spread over the table around her computer. She was attempting to construct her CV, with little success. After yet another failed attempt she savagely tore up the paper and threw it onto the growing pile at her feet "Damn! Damn! Damn!" She dropped her head in her hands. Perhaps it was the weather that made her feel so low. It was unseasonably cold. The rain had been falling steadily all day and a sullen grey sky blocked out every ray of sunshine.

Jez shivered.

"To hell with it! Who cares if it's June? I'm cold and I'm going to light the fire," she declared to the empty room.

At first the cold chimney smoked, leaving a grey fog in the air of the little dining room, but at last the fire was blazing steadily. Jez felt a glow of pride as she sat back and admired the fireplace. It was nearly all her own work. The stone had cleaned up beautifully and she had polished the oak crossbeam until it glowed. The plaster behind the fire was blackened with the soot of ages but she had decided to leave it, thinking it would be wasted effort to re-plaster, only to have it go black again after the first winter. She threw on a couple of logs and watched the flames crackle around them. There was definitely something cheering about a real fire.

Jez battled on with her CV until she was sufficiently satisfied with her notes to write them up on her laptop.

"Now, let's find a job."

She picked up one of the papers and flicked through to the Appointments Section, but as she turned the pages, a large photograph in the business section caught her attention. There was an article about the ongoing talks between CME and an American communications company, but the only picture the paper could come up with showed Piers promoting his string of hotels. The camera seemed to dwell lovingly on the dazzlingly beautiful woman clinging to his arm.

Suddenly, all the longing she had suppressed for months burst through her defences. She was back in the lounge of the Old Sun. Piers had offered her everything, and she had turned him down. He had told her he would not bother her, and she had not seen or heard from him since. The only news she gleaned of him now was the odd mention in the financial columns of the papers, and an occasional picture at some charity gala, or a social function to promote one of his businesses—yet every picture showed him with a different girl. That hurt enough, but she wondered how she would feel if he started appearing with the same girl in every photo. It had to happen. He was too attractive to stay free forever.

The crackle of logs in the fireplace broke into her misery.

One of the logs was in imminent danger of rolling off the fire so she picked up the fire tongs to put it back into the flames. Kneeling before the fire, she noticed a crack had appeared in the old black plaster behind the grate. She sighed with frustration. Perhaps they should have knocked everything away and replaced the plaster, but it had all seemed solid enough and she had been impatient to get it finished.

Jez picked up the poker and tapped gently at the plaster. It sounded hollow, loose. The next moment a large chunk crashed down onto the hearth.

"Oh shit!" She jumped back and checked the rug anxiously for burning embers. Then she knelt before the fire again and looked up to inspect the damage.

Chapter Twenty-seven

Where the blackened plaster had fallen away there was now a lighter patch exposed, about half a metre square, and in the centre was a small iron door.

Jez stared. She guessed it was some sort of oven, but the latch had been removed and the whole thing had been plastered over. Gently she traced the poker around the edge of the old door. The mortar used to seal it crumbled away at a touch. Using the poker and the tongs as levers, it took only a few moments to prise open the door. The hinges creaked loudly in protest.

A momentary break in the clouds brightened the room and a shaft of watery sunlight fell on the fireplace, illuminating the cavity like a stage spotlight. Inside was a small, greyish shape— a book, perhaps, or a small box. As the sunlight died away, Jez reached in, making sure she did not touch the hot edges of the cavity. With a shaking hand she took out the grey object.

It was not a book, but some sort of wallet, with a cover of tooled leather. She sank to the floor, staring at her find. The initials SM were carved in the leather, next to the intricate carving of a coat of arms, almost too faint to make out the detail. Carefully she eased the wallet open. It was grey and dusty with age, but surprisingly supple. Inside were several folded yellow sheets of paper, tied with a faded green ribbon.

With trembling fingers Jez slipped off the ribbon and opened out the sheets to expose the now familiar sloping characters.

Lilac Cottage

30th April 1777

My dear Lord,

It is ten years to the day since you departed this earth, and for the first time I am too unwell to go to church to pray for you. The doctor has confined me to my bed and I have no other occupation than my pen. It gives me such solace to write these words to you, even when I know you can never read them. They will remain hidden in this wallet that you gave me, so long ago now. Such a small gift, but I treasure it as I never did the jewels you bought for me. I wish you could know how much I miss you and all your little kindnesses, such as supplying me with the scented tea you knew I favoured. Even though you kept to your word and stayed away from Lilac Cottage, it was a comfort to know you still cared for me. I pray for your widow, too: she has adhered to your wish that I should be left in peace, but brings shame on your family name. You always considered yourself a dissolute soul, but your Countess is more than your equal. Even in my quiet village there is talk of her scandalous living, of her lovers and extravagances. Still I pray for her soul. A messenger brought me news this week that I, too, am now a widow. Thomas was carried off with a fever, a swift virulent illness that they tell me took him within three days. The news gave me pause to consider my own demise and I asked Parson Tully to call. I wish to give him instructions for my burial. Thanks to your generosity, I have funds enough for this. I will ask to be buried here in Luxbury. I have no wish to be buried with Thomas at Burford. He would not want me there, and since I cannot lie with you, my dearest Richard, I hope to find peace here, where I have lived under your protection for so long.

10th June 1777

Today my son Thomas came to call. He has grown into such a fine man and he tells me he has three fine sons of his own, plus a daughter—oh Richard, only think of it, I am a grandmother! All these years and I have never known it, and quite possibly I would still be in ignorance if it had not been for the fever which obliged my husband to make his peace with his Maker and to confess to his son that I am still alive. Young Thomas tells me that until that time, less than two days before his father's death, he had always believed that I was dead. Most of the old servants were turned off when I left, those that were retained had been sworn to secrecy and over the years I had been erased from memory. I wept when I heard this, Richard—not for myself, for those tears were shed long ago, but for my children, my babies left without a mother. Yet for all that I cannot find it in me to condemn Thomas for his actions. They were brought about by my betrayal, after all, but once young Thomas knew the truth he sought me out, wrote to ask my permission to call and has been here, in person. Our meeting was constrained, at first, but Thomas is so good, so kind, that he has awakened all those feelings of love so natural in a mother.

February 1779

Young Thomas is now a regular visitor to my little cottage, with his lovely family. Little Jenny is also a mother now and has brought her little ones to see me. I love them all, especially the youngest, baby Margaret. Such a dainty babe with the look of her mother at that age. Richard, my dear, I have decided to bequeath Lilac Cottage to Margaret, and it shall be handed down thereafter in the female line. I have spoken to young Thomas and he is quite content at that—his own family are already well provided for. The dear boy has even asked me to go back with him to Burford, to live with them all at the big house, but I cannot. I have lived here for more than thirty years, and I cannot leave here now—how would your spirit ever find me? Oh, my dear, dear Richard. We have both paid for our sins a thousand-fold and surely God in his mercy will let us find peace together in the next world. Wait for me there, Richard. I do believe that I shall not be long now.

There was a post script, hastily scrawled at the bottom of this final letter, but Jez was familiar with the handwriting now, and the words seemed to speak to her from the page.

> *The doctor says it was a seizure. I believe it is God's will. He is summoning me to him and I pray I will find you there. Parson Tully has been to sit with me and together we sought forgiveness. But Richard, with the end so near why am I now so filled with doubt? Was it so wrong, what we did? Was it not more cruel of me to deny our love all these years? Dear God forgive me, I find now that I cannot regret or repent my love for you. It has proved too strong, too enduring, and should any child confess to me such a love as we have shared, I should counsel them to seek their happiness on this earth...*

Jez sat for a long time on the floor with the letters before her. It was only when a tear dropped onto the fragile paper that she came out of her reverie. Looking at the sooty cavity that had yielded the letters, she could imagine Sarah hiding the wallet there and sealing the door. She had never intended the letters to be read—or had she? Strange that the message they contained was so relevant to Jez's own life.

Carefully Jez folded the letters, slid the ribbon over them and put them back in the wallet. Then she picked up the telephone. First she tried the mobile number and left a message on the answering service for Piers to ring her. Then she tried Cordeaux House, but there was no reply, only an answerphone—an electronic imitation of Piers' smooth tones. It brought her little comfort.

§

The journey home on the underground took Drina McIntosh forty minutes, time that she usually spent reading the latest paperback bestseller, but tonight she couldn't concentrate. She stared at her own reflection in the dirty window and clutched at her bag. She had felt uneasy all day, yet there was nothing she could pinpoint—work at the office had been finished smoothly, all the loose ends tied up. She had spoken to Piers briefly by phone in the morning and had left the file with information on his USA trip on the desk for him to collect when he returned to Cordeaux House that evening. Everything as normal, so why was she so anxious?

At home she tried to put work out of her mind, yet still the doubts nagged her. At seven thirty she rang the apartment number but immediately the recorded message clicked in. She knew she had switched the phone line over to the top-floor apartment before she left the office—Piers must have put it back, a habit of his when he did not want to be disturbed. A vision of her boss rose in her mind. Not the immaculate figure featured in the society pages but Piers as she had seen him the past few weeks, a strained, haunted air about him that she had never known before. She picked up her organiser, searching for a number.

Jez jumped when the phone's ringtones broke the silence of the cottage. She frowned, unable at first to place the voice.

"Jessica Skelton? It's Drina McIntosh here—you remember me? Mr. Cordeaux's PA. I picked up your message from Piers' voice mail just before I left the office. He is due to leave for the States tomorrow." There was a pause, uncharacteristic of the super-efficient Ms. McIntosh, Jez thought. "I know he's at Cordeaux House but he's not answering his phone or picking up his messages. I thought *you* might be able to contact him. If

239

you went to Cordeaux House."

"You mean in person? But I'm in Luxbury—that's more than two hours' drive—"

The voice at the other end of the line cut her short.

"Miss Skelton—Jessica, I have worked for Piers Cordeaux for more than five years. He's never said anything to me, but when you work closely with someone you *know* when something is wrong. If you have anything you want to say to him, I suggest you get yourself to London and do it now. You may not get another chance."

Icy fingers stroked Jez's spine.

"What do you mean?"

"I—I'm not sure, but Piers is not himself. Call it women's intuition—but don't tell anyone you ever heard me utter such words! I don't think he'd let *me* help him, but you might be able to."

"Right. I'm on my way. Drina?"

"Yes?"

"Thank you."

Chapter Twenty-eight

Jez walked back into the dining room to collect her shoulder bag. The plaster was still scattered over the carpet and the table littered with papers. It would have to wait. She put a guard in front of the fire and turned off the computer, then, after a moment's hesitation, she carefully picked up the wallet, the old leather feeling warm beneath her fingers. She slid it into her bag and ran out to her car.

The battery was completely dead.

She slumped in her seat. Perhaps Drina was wrong and she was wasting her time going to London. But somehow she didn't think so. Her impression of Drina McIntosh did not lead her to believe the woman was given to fanciful imaginings. If she had taken the trouble to ring then she must be seriously worried.

Jez locked the car and ran down the High Street towards the taxi-rank. It was raining steadily but she did not consider going back to the cottage for a raincoat or an umbrella. She only wanted to get to London, and she prayed there would be a through-train from Filchester.

A little over two hours later Jez was standing outside the locked gates of Cordeaux House. She tried the intercom but there was no reply. She leaned against the gate, her hands gripping the bars, the sharp edges of the iron roses pressing into her palms. The rain trickled relentlessly from her hair and down her neck, but it was more than the rain down her back that was making her shiver—it was all so familiar. She stared through the bars at the floodlit portico of the old house, the elegant fluted pillars of the entrance, topped with the grand pediment engraved with the date of 1790.

She shook the gates and almost screamed aloud with anger and frustration. Piers was in there, she was sure of it, but how to get in if he would not answer the intercom?

As she looked at the security keypad embedded in one of the gate pillars, something stirred in her memory. What was it Piers had told her—the house had been finished earlier than the portico, and he had used the original date as the code for the keypad. She pulled her purse from the shoulder bag and found the pass card Drina had given her when she had visited Cordeaux House. Thank God she was so bad at throwing things out.

Now, if she could only remember that date. She felt a tug of wry humour as the year came into her head—1746, the same year that Sarah had left her husband. Her wet fingers slipped on the metal keys but at the second attempt she heard a reassuring buzz, and once she had dragged her pass card through the sensor, the locks of the big gates rasped back.

Jez slipped into the courtyard, carefully closing the gates behind her. The locks slid back into position, but she was already heading towards the house. She gave a thankful sigh as the same combination opened the main door. She was standing in the marble hall of Cordeaux House. The whole of the ground floor was dimly lit by emergency lamps. The air was chill, and she felt as if she was being watched. Her eyes moved to the security camera high on the wall. If she was challenged, how would she explain her presence?

She tried the lift button, but there was only silence, no

sounds of anything happening there. She tried it again, but the continuing silence convinced her that to reach Piers' apartment she would have to go through the main offices. Shaking a little, she used her pass card to open the glass doors, then walked through reception and up the main staircase. The low lighting robbed everything of colour, but at least she could see her way. She carried on up the second flight of stairs, but found the doors at the top locked.

Quickly she returned to the first-floor landing, trying to recall the layout of the house from her previous visit. She must stay calm, and think logically. She remembered walking through the boardroom to Piers' own office. There had been another staircase on the far side, leading to the upper floor.

Jez swallowed hard. It was eerily quiet and the very stillness of the building made her nervous. There was no going back now. She opened one of the big double doors to the boardroom. It was in darkness, except for the oblongs of pale grey on the ceiling, reflections from the streetlights outside the windows. She hesitated. She could just make out the doors on the far side of the room. *It isn't far*, she told herself sternly. *It won't take a minute, and if I leave this door open to let in a little light...*

Jez stepped into the room, keeping close to the windows and the reassuring view of the street outside. She became aware of an icy chill. Her damp clothes were uncomfortable and her hair was wet and heavy on her shoulders. She heard the faint tinkling of glass, like wind-chimes. She realised it was the glass lusters on the huge chandeliers. They were moving gently, so there had to be a draught coming from somewhere.

By the time Jez reached the far doors, the tingling in her spine was almost unbearable. She felt that someone was behind her. Common sense told her that was impossible, and naked fear prevented her from looking over her shoulder. With a trembling hand she opened one of the doors leading into Piers' office. It was even darker than the boardroom, the blinds at the windows cutting out any light from the street. She smelled the familiar scent of leather and paper—only natural, she told herself, since it was the old library.

Resolutely she fixed her eyes on the dim outline of the opposite door. The service stairs were through there. She moved forward.

Halfway across the room Jez hesitated, sure that she was not alone. She strained her eyes to pierce the darkness, but everything was black. Her throat felt dry and when she tried to speak she could only manage a whisper.

"Piers, is that you?"

"I knew you would come back."

She became aware of his presence close behind her, and recognised with relief the familiar hint of sandalwood cologne. She turned within the reassuring circle of his arms and leaned her cheek against his shoulder.

"Oh God, I was so frightened! Stupid of me, I know." She tried to laugh. "What's this you're wearing? Feels like velvet... Is it a dressing gown?"

He did not answer, but kissed her instead. She responded hungrily, admitting to herself for the first time how lonely she had been.

"Oh how I've missed you!" she whispered, when the long kiss ended.

"I'll never let you go again, my dear one. I prayed that you would come back to me, that you would forgive me. Oh, Sarah."

Jez froze. Her hand was resting lightly on his chest, and she moved her fingers until smooth velvet changed to stiff ruffled lace at his throat. Fighting down her panic, she raised her head. His figure was merely a black shape outlined against the darkness but it *had* to be Piers—the shape of his head, the strong jaw line—and that kiss, she could not be mistaken! Her hand continued to move, up over an embroidered collar and to his hair, but instead of the sleek, short cut, her fingers traced long hair pulled back and confined at the nape of his neck with a thin velvet ribbon.

"Oh my God!" She pushed him away.

"Don't be afraid of me, Sarah—I give you my word I will not hurt you again."

"This is madness!" she muttered aloud. "I must be dreaming."

Yet the darkness and the figure in front of her were very real. He reached for her again but she stepped back.

"Who are you?" she demanded, but she knew. Illogical as it was, she knew this man.

"You have come back to me, Sarah. Tell me you love me."

"I'm not Sarah, I'm Jez."

Some detached part of her brain told her this could not be happening. If it was not Piers, it must be an intruder. So why was it she felt no fear now, only an enormous sympathy? She began to move away.

"Oh no." His hand shot out, taking her wrist in an iron grip. "You won't leave me again."

"Oh, you poor thing! Sarah's dead, Richard, a long time ago." The grip did not slacken, and she put her free hand over the fingers on her wrist, feeling the flesh of his hand, smooth and hard. Real. "She's gone, Richard. She's waiting for you."

He did not seem to hear her. He pulled her to him, drawing her into his arms.

"Sarah, tell me. Say you love me."

She could not resist him—physically he was too strong for her, she knew that, but something within her wanted to yield to him. She felt reality slipping away. It would be so easy to give in, to stop fighting. She had to try.

"No, Richard. It's not *me* you want. *I'm* not Sarah!"

As he pulled her closer, the blackness seemed to grow around them. Jez sobbed and summoned up her remaining energy to push against him, holding him away from her.

"Wait—wait, Richard! I have a letter for you—letters from Sarah." She reached into her shoulder bag and pulled out the leather case. "Take it, Richard—it's your wallet—the one you gave Sarah, do you remember?" She pushed it against him, adding softly, "She *did* love you, Richard, and she forgave you."

He put one hand on the wallet.

"Sarah?"

"Read them. Read her letters."

His grip on her wrist slackened and Jez was able to pull away. She wanted to turn and run, but could not tear her eyes away from the blackness, from his black shape.

She moved back slowly. Another few steps and the door to the service stairs was within reach. She stretched one hand behind her, feeling for the door while her eyes remained fixed on the black figure. It was so dark her straining eyes could not be sure there was anything there any more.

Her trembling fingers closed on the handle and in one swift movement she wrenched the door open and ran out, slamming the door behind her. She found herself on a small landing in the cold glare of an electric light. She flew up the stairs to the executive suite, stumbling as she forced her trembling legs to carry her upwards to the heavy panelled door at the top.

Chapter Twenty-nine

Jez knocked urgently on the door to Piers' apartment. There was no response. She knocked again. He *had* to be in. Fearfully she glanced back down the stairs but nothing moved. The house was silent, save for the rain pattering against the windows. Fear still tingled down her spine. She leaned against the door, hammering on it with the flat of her hand.

"Piers! For God's sake—let me in."

When the door opened she almost fell into Piers' arms.

"What the—?"

"Oh, thank God!"

"Jez!" Piers took her into the lounge, supporting her as her legs refused to carry her. "What's wrong? What's happened?" He gently pushed her down onto the sofa and sat beside her, keeping an arm about her shoulders, while she trembled and shivered convulsively.

She stared at him blankly, trying to think. Piers covered her hands in a warm, comforting clasp.

"All right now, love. Take a deep breath—that's right, and another..."

"There were no lights—in the library—"

"Library? Do you mean my office?"

She nodded, feeling the tears starting to her eyes. "He's

there, waiting for her."

"Who? Who's there?"

She couldn't speak, and subsided against him as the tears flowed.

"Jez, why didn't you ring me?" Piers handed her a handkerchief.

"I—I tried, but I couldn't get a reply." She wiped her eyes. "I s-still had the pass card, and remembered that you'd told me the c-combination, so I came on in..."

He ran a hand through his hair.

"I turned off my mobile, and the line here is switched back to reception." He paused. "I jammed the lift too."

"I know. I had to—to come through the offices and w-when I got to the library, it was so d-dark..." she broke off, trembling.

"Must be a fuse gone. Poor Jez, you look as if you've seen a ghost. I'll get you a brandy."

Jez sat very still, trying to control the trembling and collect her thoughts. Here in Piers' well-lit apartment with its creamy modern décor, she found it hard to remember just what had happened downstairs. The incident had taken on a dreamlike quality. She looked at the red mark on her wrist—she wasn't even sure that it had not been there yesterday.

As Piers came back into the room she looked at him properly for the first time and she had to bite back a gasp of surprise at his ragged appearance. The usually sleek hair was tousled and although he was still wearing his suit trousers and white shirt, the jacket and tie had been discarded and there was at least one day's dark stubble on his face. As he drew closer, she noticed the dark circles around his eyes. She had never seen him looking so weary.

He was carrying two glasses, one of which he handed to

her.

She sipped gratefully at the brandy, thankful for its warmth inside her.

"Is that better?"

"Yes, thank you. Is there—*could* there be anyone else in the building?"

"I doubt it. Only a few people have full clearance, with access to the building at night. Myself, naturally, Max, my vice president, but he's in New York at the moment, and Drina. Oh, and you. Jez? What is it?"

She hesitated, wanting to say, *I think I've met one of your ancestors*, but she could imagine his reaction to that.

Instead she said, "I thought there was—something in the library."

"You mean my office. No, it's just your imagination, love. With no lights and this rain beating against the window, I'm not surprised you were frightened. I find the room a bit gloomy myself at times—in fact, I haven't worked in there at all for the past few weeks." He put down his glass. "Why did you come tonight?"

"I heard you were going to the States."

"Yes. Tomorrow afternoon."

She glanced around. "This place is a mess—and so are you."

He laughed, but without humour. "I can't say I've given it much thought recently."

She did not look at him, but she was aware that her heart was beating very fast.

He said, "How's Harry?"

"Harry's gone. Months ago. He—he's found someone else."

"Are you sorry?"

"No, I don't think so."

"Why didn't you tell me?"

She thought of the photos in the society magazines, the beautiful women on his arm. "You—you seemed to be doing just fine without me. You're never out of the papers, always with a partner."

"It's expected of me." He paused. "For what it's worth I haven't taken any of them to bed, even though I thought I'd never see you again."

Jez thought of the earl, waiting through the centuries for Sarah. "Perhaps you come from faithful stock." She looked up to find him standing over her.

He reached down and pulled her up into his arms. "So why did you come?"

She felt suddenly very shy. "I—I thought you might need me."

"I do. How long can you stay?"

The words sent her spirits soaring. "Forever, if you'll let me."

He kissed her, the stubble on his chin scratching her face, but she did not mind that. Neither did she object when he picked her up and carried her to the bedroom, where he undressed her with infinite care and made love to her with such tenderness that finally her passion would wait no longer and she rolled on top of him and took control.

Afterwards, Jez lay in the protective circle of his arms, an immense feeling of peace and happiness spreading through her. She stirred slightly and was reassured to feel his limbs wrapped around her.

"I love you," she murmured sleepily.

Piers kissed her neck. "I love you, too. Come to America with me."

"But you're leaving tomorrow."

"I'll cancel my flight and book us both on a later one."

"What would I do?"

"Well, you've finished your studies now, haven't you? You can put what you've learned into practice. I didn't just sign your in-company report, you know. I read it, too. It was very good. You've familiarised yourself with the company and you've a good understanding of where I want CME to go. You can work with me."

"But—what if I'm useless?"

"Then I'll marry you and you can stay at home and have our babies."

Jez closed her eyes, dizzy at the prospect.

"Okay." Her voice was shaky. "It's madness, but okay."

He raised himself on one elbow, looking down at her. "You will?"

She ran a hand through the hairs on his chest. No thick mat, just a few dark strands between her fingers that caused a pleasurable excitement to run down through her body.

"Yes. I'll have to make a few calls, but there's nothing that can't be changed." She hoped her mother would understand.

Piers kissed her.

"Good." He rolled over. "Are you hungry? Let's go out for something to eat."

"Piers—it's midnight!"

He kissed her again.

"What about it—unless you're Cinderella? There's always

somewhere open in London if you know where to look."

"Piers?"

"Mm?"

She touched the dark stubble on his cheek. "Is this because of *me*?"

The laughter left his eyes and he regarded her seriously. "I was beginning to wonder if there was any point in going on. For a few hours tonight it all seemed so—hopeless."

She shuddered and pulled him to her.

"Oh Piers, we came so close to losing each other!"

They showered together, then Piers tenderly wrapped her in a thick bath sheet. Jez noticed the Cordeaux crest embroidered in one corner. Its outline was vaguely familiar.

"The leather wallet! I'd forgotten about it."

Piers was busy removing two days' growth of beard from his chin and merely looked an enquiry in the mirror.

"I think I've found a connection between our families. You remember the fireplace we were uncovering at Lilac Cottage? I found a small oven at the back. The door was sealed and inside was a leather wallet, and I'm certain it has this crest upon it." She hesitated, then said shyly, "There were some letters, written by a distant relative of mine to someone called Richard."

"Richard is a family name. It was a Richard, Earl of Cordeaux, who built this house."

"Then it could be the same person. Sarah was very much in love with him, but she was already married and very religious, so she never told him. I think Richard gave her the wallet at some point, and Sarah used it to hold the letters she wrote after his death. Everything she wanted to tell him but never could."

"Sarah Methven?"

Jez stared. "Yes. How did you know?"

"I have her portrait in my office."

"That's where I dropped the wallet."

"Then we'll go out that way." He heard her gasp and smiled. "Don't worry, no ghosts will bother you while I'm here."

Chapter Thirty

They left by the service stair and, sensing her nervousness, Piers switched on all the lights, banishing every vestige of shadow. When they reached his office she hung back, clinging to his hand, and when he opened the door she could not restrain a little whimper, but instead of the inky darkness, the room was lit by the dim glow from the security lights.

"But—they weren't working!"

"Well, everything's fine now." He switched on the main lights and led her into the room. "Last time I showed you around, the pictures were away being cleaned and restored. That's Sarah, over the fireplace, and on the side wall is a full-length picture of Richard Cordeaux. Bit of a wild lad in his youth, I understand, but he later reformed and spent a lot of his fortune on charitable works."

Jez studied the painting. There was no mistaking the likeness between Richard and Piers.

"I found them in the attic when I bought the place. For years we thought Sarah was a member of the family, because of the family crest on the book she's holding. Then we found the inventory for 1767 where there's an entry for a portrait of Sarah, Lady Methven. It states it was painted when she was twenty-three. I've had it checked out—it's an original by Reynolds, like the one of Richard Cordeaux, that's a Reynolds, too. God knows how they survived there all these years without being discovered."

Jez walked closer to the fireplace and looked up at her ancestor. A young woman stared back at her, her hair pulled back from her face, after the style of the day, but the colour was the same as her own, a bright reddish brown, and the eyes staring out solemnly from the painting were the same rich green.

"I'd never noticed the resemblance, until now." Piers walked up behind her, but Jez did not take her eyes from the painting.

"That's not a book she's holding, Piers," she breathed. "It's the wallet—the one I dropped in here..." She started to look around the floor.

"This one?" Piers was pointing to his desk. The wallet was lying on the polished mahogany. It was faded and very worn, but identical to the painting.

"Yes—look, her letters are still inside..." Jez opened the wallet. "Oh—but I don't understand. I was reading them just before I came here!"

The letters had disintegrated into greying powdery fragments inside the leather wallet, with the green silk ribbon snaking amongst the dust.

"Didn't you say that you found the wallet sealed up? It may be the contact with the air that's caused the letters to disintegrate. Pity, though. I'd like to have read them."

"But they were for Richard."

"And I'm not Richard, huh?"

And I'm not Sarah, she added silently.

"Come on." Piers grinned. "It's not ghosts haunting you, my girl, it's hunger."

Jez did not reply. No point in trying to explain what she

255

didn't understand herself. She glanced up at Sarah's picture. *Thanks, Sarah.*

"Jez, are you coming?" Piers was standing by the door, his hand on the light switch.

"It's all right, Piers, you can turn off the lights now. I'm not afraid any more."

"By the way, how did you get here? Did you walk all the way?" He held open the door for her. "Your jacket's still wet."

"I had to use the train. My car wouldn't start." She skipped down the stairs beside him. "Oh, that reminds me. You remember that Porsche you wanted to give me for Christmas? Well, I really do need a new car now, so, Piers, do you think..."

About the Author

Melinda Hammond lives in an old farmhouse in the Yorkshire Pennines. Her interests include theatre and music and supporting her son's go-kart racing team—although she feels obliged to stay at home and keep the log fire burning during the winter months. She has published fourteen historical adventure romances in the UK in addition to romance novels under the pen name Sarah Mallory.

To learn more about Melinda Hammond please visit www.melindahammond.com or send an email to Melinda Hammond at melinda@melindahammond.co.uk.

His legendary spirit is restless for revenge. But the touch of one woman could change his mind—and his destiny.

Beaudry's Ghost
© *2008 Carolan Ivey*

An irresistible force.

When Jared Beaudry's restless spirit stumbles across a re-enactment of the Civil War battle in which he was murdered and mutilated, he jumps at the chance to find peace at last. Instead, his desperate leap into another man's body triggers a deadly chain of events nothing can stop.

An immovable object.

Faced with an entire re-enacting unit possessed by spirits of the dead, psychic sensitive Taylor Brannon's first instinct is to run. But she swallows her terror and stands her ground to protect her friends from a ghost who seems hell-bent on revenge and self-destruction.

Spontaneous combustion.

Jared's powerful spirit touches her in the most deeply guarded depths of her heart, and after one burning night in his arms, Taylor adds another impossible task to her list: To somehow help Beaudry's Ghost find peace. Caught up in a runaway train of events that races inevitably toward one tragic conclusion, Taylor finds herself fighting for the life—and love—of a ghost.

The cost could be her soul.

Available now in ebook and print from Samhain Publishing.

Enjoy the following excerpt from Beaudry's Ghost...

Taylor rested her Enfield across her lap and pressed her fingertips to her eyelids. She fought two days' worth of exhaustion, having decided at the last minute to join the event wearing Troy's Confederate uniform. Disagreements they'd certainly had, but she and Troy had shared a love of history and Civil War re-enacting. Taylor rested her chin on her arm, breathing in the damp-wool smell of the uniform. The others thought she wore it merely as a tribute to Troy, and had said nothing when she had shown up early that morning. She chose to let them believe that, rather than try to explain the truth.

She knew better than to fall asleep while on guard duty, but the emotional day she had endured gradually took its final toll. Her rear end settled onto the sand. The butt of her musket joined it, but she was too tired to care.

Moments later, hoof beats drummed her awake. Taylor found herself standing on the dune, watching a horse and rider streak down the beach at full gallop.

Wherever that horse had come from, it had been running a long time. Steam trailed off the animal's body, the light of the moon setting it to silver fire. That horse was flying. Its rider leaned low and listed slightly to one side, as if favoring an injured limb.

The messenger? He was early. And if he didn't turn aside very soon, he would run his horse right into the giant oak ribs of a shipwreck beached on the shore.

Taylor absently fingered the back of her newly shorn hair and frowned. He wasn't supposed to be here for another day, this messenger "warning" her unit of an approaching enemy of Union troops from the south. And something else was wrong.

This rider rode down the beach from the north.

"But...he's coming from the wrong direction..."

She realized she'd spoken aloud when the rider's body jerked. With a low moan, he pulled the horse to a rearing stop directly opposite her on the beach. The horse, clearly not happy about being made to stand, pranced in an ankle-deep tidal pool.

Taylor strained to see if the rider wore a uniform. She observed his the slumped posture and thought maybe he and the horse weren't part of this re-enactment of the Civil War Battle of Roanoke.

"Hey! Are you hurt? Do you need help?"

With a Herculean effort, the he straightened, turned the trembling, sweaty horse in her direction and approached at a walk. As they closed in on her, she heard the horse's labored snorts and something else...

With each breath, the rider emitted a gurgling, inarticulate grunt. The sound carried with it the weight of a weariness she could sense but not fathom.

The offshore wind grew louder in her ears, and Taylor reached up to grab her hat before it flew off. At that moment she realized the physical wind remained steady.

But a roaring force pushed at her carefully walled-off soul.

Taylor's fingers alternately tightened and loosened on the musket she held, a faintly caressing gesture as if she rubbed a magic lamp. Conjuring up someone. Or something. Like courage.

The horse caught her scent. It reared and spun, and in the rising moonlight Taylor finally caught a clear glimpse of the rider.

He wore a blue uniform. And he was...

"Oh my God."

Her chest muscles spasmed, leaving no space for her to draw air. Sheer reflex brought her musket to her shoulder and she aimed...at what? A figure whose bound stump of a left arm oozed blood. He held it tightly to his side while he controlled the horse with his right. Soaked rags acted as a tourniquet to what was left of his right leg, but his every effort to stay in the saddle forced out more and more blood.

And the man—she guessed it was a man—had an enormous, gaping slash through his throat.

She was aiming at a dead man, her musket loaded with a useless blank. Fired, it would make a grand noise, and that was about all.

"And they say Beaudry's ghost rides the Outer Banks to this day, looking for his lost body parts...and for revenge..."

That gurgling noise she'd heard was the sound of a man whose throat had been cut. Clear through.

Taylor grit her teeth. Those ghost stories were coming back to haunt her in a big way. Her rational mind objected and rejected as fast as her eyes fed it the irrational sight. The carefully tended wall round her soul cracked, and her demons screamed through. An answering scream clawed for space in her throat along with the hardtack and beans she'd eaten hours ago.

Trembling, she braced herself as if leaning against that wall. A dream. Of course. She was dreaming this whole thing. She'd expected to have a few nightmares—even visions—before this event was over, but nothing like this. She'd only fallen asleep at her post and—

Oh, God, it's moving toward me!

Clouds of steam streaked from the horse's nostrils, and as it moved closer she saw the white rings around its black eyes. Taylor closed hers.

"You aren't real. You...aren't...real!" she muttered through clenched teeth. A breath of air whisked right through her body in a distinctive front-to-back direction, leaving her with the odd feeling that she'd just exposed her deepest vulnerability to a lover. Taylor went perfectly still. *Somebody tell me this thing just didn't pass right through me!*

"Aw, the hell with this!" Facing cannon and musket fire was one thing. Facing this ghastly evidence that a dark otherworld indeed existed on another plane, and that the two planes sometimes crossed, was quite another.

Taylor dropped her Tennessee pride in the sand behind her and fled down the steep slope of the dune. Gasping, sliding, stumbling, she hit bottom and headed for camp and for help.

Stupid! Stupid! I should have fired... Troy would have at least fired...

GREAT cheap FUN

Discover eBooks!
THE FASTEST WAY TO GET THE HOTTEST NAMES

Get your favorite authors on your favorite reader, long before they're
out in print! Ebooks from Samhain go wherever you go, and work with
whatever you carry—Palm, PDF, Mobi, and more.

Printed in the United States
149321LV00001B/96/P